FOUND

FOUND

S. A. BODEEN

SQUARE
FISH

FEIWEL AND FRIENDS
NEW YORK

SQUARE
FISH

An imprint of Macmillan Publishing Group, LLC
175 Fifth Avenue, New York, NY 10010
mackids.com

Square Fish and the Square Fish logo are trademarks of Macmillan and
are used by Feiwel and Friends under license from Macmillan.

Our books may be purchased in bulk for promotional, educational, or business
use. Please contact your local bookseller or the Macmillan Corporate
and Premium Sales Department at (800) 221-7945 ext. 5442 or by
e-mail at MacmillanSpecialMarkets@macmillan.com.

Library of Congress Cataloging-in-Publication Data is available.

ISBN 978-1-250-02784-9 (paperback)   ISBN 978-1-250-13417-2 (ebook)

Originally published in the United States by Feiwel and Friends
First Square Fish edition, 2018
Book designed by Anna Booth
Square Fish logo designed by Filomena Tuosto

1   3   5   7   9   10   8   6   4   2

AR: 3.7

For Karen, my trusty sidekick through many an adventure, both foreign and domestic

1

Sarah Robinson was in a tunnel of trouble, long and dark with no light whatsoever at the end. Worse, there was absolutely no one to lead her out.

For three days and nights, her family had been marooned on Shipwreck Island with their skipper's dog, Ahab, and Cash, a girl they found on the beach at the end of the second day. In that short time, Sarah had been chased by giant coconut crabs, nearly eaten by a shark on legs, and taken prisoner—albeit briefly—by an alien named Leo.

As if that wasn't enough, her stepmother, Yvonna, was very ill in the early stages of pregnancy. Yes, Sarah and her stepbrothers, Marco and Nacho, would soon be connected forever by a new brother or sister. (And Sarah hadn't even had the time to figure out for sure how she felt about *that*.) Plus, the last time she saw her father, John, he had been turned into a human freeze pop by Leo in a strange and possibly deadly experiment.

One would think things were as bad as they could possibly be. But Sarah knew that anyone who thought that would be mistaken.

Because, on the dawn of their fourth day on the island, she woke on the beach beside the fire to find herself confronted by Fox, the man who had commandeered the sailboat belonging to Cash's grandfather, Sarge. Fox was on the hunt for a missing treasure, one that he may have left on the island. And he would stop at nothing to recover it.

With Fox only feet away, Sarah stood in the sand and held tight to Ahab's collar with trembling hands. She stared out at Sarge's sailboat floating in the lovely blue lagoon. If only she could get out there. Then she could call for help, maybe find a way to make Yvonna feel better, and get her family off the island. But there was no chance of any of that happening, not after what she'd told Fox.

When he'd stopped here on Sarge's sailboat tour, Fox hadn't realized this island was the one he was after. It looked different because Leo and his alien grandfather had changed the appearance of the island in many ways that made it unrecognizable to Fox as the place where he had been marooned and hidden his treasure.

But there had been one landmark, one thing that would prove beyond a doubt that this was the island where'd he'd left the treasure: the face rock. Sarah had told him the truth, that she had seen it. And now she had no choice but to take him there.

But what would happen when they reached the spot and Fox realized that his treasure wasn't there?

Her only hope was to stall him, lead him around until they met up with her dad and Marco. *If* the alien, Leo—who had proven to be untrustworthy in the short time they'd known him—had done as he promised and unfrozen her father.

Sarah crossed her fingers and whispered, "Dad, please, *please* be on your way back."

"You! Girly," Fox called to Sarah as he held a struggling, wide-eyed Cash. "Help me tie her up."

Sarah swallowed a gasp. "Why do you have to tie her up?"

"She's not coming with us. And I don't trust her here alone." He frowned. "In fact . . ."

He grabbed Sarah.

She tried to get away, but his firm grip was too strong. And too painful.

Ahab barked.

Fox bent a leg to kick him, and Sarah screeched, "No!"

Fox scowled. "You tie him to a tree or I will."

"Fine."

Fox released her and she led Ahab over to a palm tree. Fox gave her a length of rope and hovered over them, but she kept herself between the man and the dog.

Ahab whined and licked Sarah's cheek.

She buried her face in his fur and whispered, "I don't know if you can understand me, but you need to get away. You need to run and hide. Like, right now. Boy, do you understand—"

With a yip, Ahab tugged away from Sarah and ran for the trees.

Fox raised the gun.

"No!" Sarah dropped the rope and plowed into Fox, nearly knocking him over.

He shoved her back and regained his footing.

Sarah whirled around, looking for the dog. But Ahab was gone. At least one of them got away.

Fox snatched up the length of rope and grabbed her

arm. "No more messing around!" He dragged her over to a palm tree and tied the girls' hands together. Sarah found herself stuck to the tree with Cash as Fox strode off toward the dinghy on shore.

She shot a glance toward the monkey pod trees, where her younger stepbrother, Nacho, peered over the edge of the platform. "Maybe he can free us."

As if her words carried that far, he slid a leg over the edge and began to lower himself.

"No!" whispered Cash. "What if Fox catches him?"

Sarah said, "I think there's time."

Nacho quickly dropped to the ground and ran toward them, sticking close to the shelter of the trees to stay hidden.

Fox dragged the dinghy into the water and began rowing back to the sailboat.

Nacho reached them, gasping a bit. "Are you okay?"

"We're tied to a tree," said Cash. "What do you think?"

Nacho dropped to his knees behind the tree, and Sarah felt his fingers fumble with the rope. "It's so tight. Do you have a knife?"

Sarah rolled her eyes. "No." Marco had one, but he probably took it with him.

As Nacho kept working on the knots, Fox reached

the sailboat. Two more people climbed into the small craft.

"Sarge!" said Cash.

The dinghy was heading back to shore.

"Why would he bring your grandpa here?" Sarah frowned.

Cash grinned. "I don't care! I'm just glad he is."

Sarah said, "Nacho, you'd better hurry."

"It's too tight!" He pulled on the rope around Sarah's wrists.

"Ow! Careful."

The small craft drew nearer.

"It's no use, Nacho," said Sarah. "You need to go."

Nacho said, "I can do this."

"You can't let him catch you."

"But I want to help!"

"Getting tied up yourself isn't going to help *any-body*." Sarah realized she sounded bossy. So she tried a never-before-used, caring-older-stepsister voice. "Nacho, just get back to the platform and stay out of sight."

Nacho moved around to her side of the tree.

Sarah rustled up a smile that she hoped looked genuine. "It'll be okay."

He huffed. "Fine." Nacho jogged back toward the monkey pod tree.

Sarah wished he could have managed the knots.

The dinghy reached the beach.

The third passenger was a woman in a white pant-suit and oversize black sunglasses. Her short dark hair didn't move a stitch in the ocean breeze, and her large, blue bejeweled necklace sparkled in the sun. She cra-dled a yappy white dog in her pale arms. "Is that the woman you told me about?" asked Sarah.

"Miss Blackstone." Cash scrunched up her nose. "She's as nasty as Fox."

"That seems impossible," mumbled Sarah.

Fox and Sarge dragged the dinghy ashore, out of the reach of the waves licking the sand. Cash's grand-father walked in front of the other two, sweat glistening on his bald head, tattoos up and down his dark, muscu-lar arms. His eyes narrowed at the sight of Cash tied up. "If you hurt her—"

Cash called out, "Sarge, I'm fine!"

Sarah whispered, "You might want to leave out the fact that you were blind up until a few minutes ago."

Fox shoved Sarge. He landed on his knees, and his gaze quickly scanned his granddaughter up and down. "Are you hurt?"

Cash shook her head. "I'm okay now that you're here."

Fox growled, "This isn't a reunion. Little missy here"—he tilted his head at Sarah—"is gonna take me where I need to go."

Sarge took a long look at Sarah. "Are you alone?"

Sarah wished she could tell him the truth, that her dad and Marco were on their way. At least, she hoped so. Instead, she simply shook her head and gestured toward Yvonna, who lay on the blanket in the sand where Fox had left her. "My stepmom."

Sarge glanced that way. "What's wrong with her?"

"She's really sick," said Sarah.

"So just the two of you?" he asked.

"Yes." Sarah hoped that Nacho would remain out of sight.

"Enough chitchat." Fox flipped open a jackknife. Sun glinted off the sharp, shiny blade.

Sarah gasped.

Fox pinched Sarah's elbow in his fingers and hauled her and Cash to their feet. Sarah shut her eyes as he sliced the rope between her and Cash and only opened them when she was sure he was done and wasn't going to cut her.

He tied Sarge to Cash and then to the tree. Fox held out the gun to Miss Blackstone.

The woman hadn't said a word but wore a heavy look of disdain that required none. She sighed heavily and shifted the dog to one arm. Then she gingerly took the firearm with her free hand, which sported long red nails. Her silence broke in a loud, nasally voice. "Laird, you know how much I hate these stupid islands." She lifted one gold-high-heel-sandaled foot. Sand trickled out. "This had *better* be the one."

"Bettina, please." Fox sighed. "All you have to do is wait here until I come back with the treasure. Then we'll leave and put this whole thing behind us."

Sarah couldn't help but notice he hadn't mentioned any of *them*. What would happen when he got the treasure? He needed Sarge to sail the boat. Would he take only Sarge and Cash, leave the rest of them there? Usually in the movies, the bad guys didn't want to leave any witnesses.

Sarah bit her lip. There were too many unknowns. She could *not* let Fox get the treasure.

His mouth turned up at Sarah, a leering, creepy smile that sent a shiver down her spine. "You ready?"

Sarah knew she had to stall. "Shouldn't we bring some water?" she asked.

Fox frowned. "How far is it?"

"A ways." Sarah had to buy enough time for Marco to free her father. "A *long* ways. Rugged terrain." For good measure, she added, "*Very* rugged."

Fox glanced around. "I don't remember anything but even ground."

Sarah cocked her head. "Do you remember these trees?"

"No, actually, I *don't*." Fox narrowed his eyes at her. "Maybe you're pulling my leg about the face rock."

Sarah sucked in a breath.

Fox was not someone to play around with.

She quickly shook her head. "No, it's real. We saw it." The words were out before she could stop them and she hoped he didn't catch her slip.

No such luck.

"*We?*" He looked from Sarah to Cash. "You both saw it?"

Sarah caught Cash's eye, but not in time. Cash said, "Not me."

Sarah quickly pointed at Yvonna. "Before she got sick we did some exploring."

Fox seemed to relax a little. "Well, get some water then and we'll be on our way."

Sarah jogged over to the fire to grab a couple of water

bottles. On her way, she snuck a glance at the platform, but didn't see Nacho. He was probably staying out of sight. She knelt beside the fire and pretended to fumble in a bag of supplies with her left hand while she scrawled a note in the sand with her right.

Don't let her see you.

She hoped Nacho would find the message and not try to be a hero. Sarah stood up, holding two bottles of water. Hopefully Leo would stick to his word, continue to be their ally, and Marco would return with her dad. They would free Sarge and Cash, rescue them all from Fox, and they could finally get off the island.

Until then, she'd have to get Fox away from there and hope her plan worked. Slowly she headed back to the others.

Fox took Miss Blackstone's elbow. "Let's find you a spot over here in the sand, Bettina."

"More sand?" Miss Blackstone yanked her elbow back. "No thank you." She plopped down under a tree a few yards away from Cash and Sarge. "This had better be the island, Laird. This had just *better* be the one."

"It is, Bettina. I swear." Fox held up the jackknife toward Sarah.

She froze as the blade came closer and closer to her face.

"I don't take to no funny business, girly."

She shook her head.

Fox folded the blade and stuffed the knife into the pocket of his cargo shorts. "Lead the way."

Sarah tried to calm down as she set off down the beach, thinking, Please, please let this work. . . .

2

Marco tried to get a deep breath as he and John trudged along in the sand under the rapidly warming morning sun. He got a better grip on the silver container of food that Leo had given him. Everyone at the beach would be happy to see it.

But what was happening back at their beach? Had the people on Sarge's boat come ashore? What if they'd hurt his mom or Nacho? Or Sarah or Cash?

He shot a sideways glance at his stepfather. John still seemed slightly dazed, even though nearly half an hour had passed since Leo released him from the module. Now that he was free, he should snap out of it soon, at least Marco hoped so. There was no telling what they might encounter once they arrived at the beach. And he hadn't exactly been truthful. Maybe it was time. "My mom—"

John stumbled as he took his eyes off the sand. He righted himself. "Is she okay?"

Marco clenched and unclenched his free hand. Things were already tense. Did he really want to add to it? "She isn't feeling well."

John stopped walking and faced him. "What's wrong?"

"Nothing. I mean . . ." Marco shrugged. "She said this is normal, that she gets sick every time."

"Every time what?" John frowned.

Marco had no choice but to tell him. "She's having a baby."

His stepfather's mouth fell open and his eyes grew big behind his glasses. "Are you sure?"

That wasn't exactly the reaction of someone who had just gotten happy news. In fact, it was worrying. Marco wasn't yet sure how he felt about getting a new brother or sister, but shouldn't John be pleased? Maybe John didn't want a baby. What would his mom do when she found out?

"Yes," said Marco. "I'm *sure*."

John grinned and shot both fists straight up above

his head. "Woo!" He grabbed Marco by both arms. "This is wonderful!"

Good. His stepfather was okay with the news. Marco grinned and held up his palm. "But you have to listen."

John still wore a huge smile. "Okay."

"Mom's *really* not feeling well. She said that last time she got so ill she had to go to the hospital."

John's expression turned somber. "We need to get off this island."

Marco said, "I think there's a way."

"How? Tell me as we go." John took off with huge strides.

Marco jogged and caught up. "Cash's grandfather is back."

"With his boat?" John's eyes lit up. "That's terrific!"

"Not really." Marco shook his head. "Those people are still with him. The ones that stranded Cash. The boat had just showed up in the lagoon when Leo and I left."

"You left Sarah and your mom?"

"Well, yeah. And Nacho and Cash are there too."

"You left all of them?"

"I had to."

John stopped. "How could you do that?"

"I had no choice! We had to go back and get you out so you could help!" Marco's hands became fists as he tried to explain that he *didn't* simply abandon everyone. "Sarah ran down to the beach, they'd already seen her. She *had* to stay. And they knew Cash was there. And Mom—"

"What?" John snapped.

"I couldn't move her." A lump formed in his throat. Spoken out loud, his actions did sound lame. Maybe he *shouldn't* have left. Frustrated, he tried one last time to defend himself. "You weren't there! I did what I thought was the best thing to do at the time."

John's words were softer. "Oh, Marco, of course you did. I should have been there." John squeezed Marco's shoulder. "You did good, okay?" He stared at Marco for a moment. "Are you much of a runner?"

"Fastest on my soccer team." Marco's shoulders slumped. "At home, I mean. In Texas." Which wasn't home anymore.

"You know, we *do* have soccer in California. My company sponsors a traveling team."

"For real?" Marco stood up straight.

"Yes." John glanced down the beach.

"Are you a runner?" asked Marco.

"Every day but Sunday." John grinned. "Let's pick it up now, shall we? We'll talk soccer when we're on that boat and headed home."

Buoyed by the possibilities, Marco tucked the silver container under one arm and jogged beside his stepfather. But the deep sand soon slowed them down.

John veered toward the water.

"We better stay up here!" called Marco.

"We can move faster on the harder sand."

"Yeah, but—" Was it worth mentioning the shark-odile? They were making good time and would be off that dangerous stretch of sand soon. Marco decided to keep his mouth shut as they kept moving.

They rounded a corner.

John was a few steps in front and stopped.

Marco nearly ran into him. "What?"

John stood there, stiff and still.

Marco wondered whether being frozen had affected him more than he thought. Maybe they shouldn't have been running.

But then his stepfather muttered, "What in the world . . . ?"

Marco leaned out and looked around him. "Oh no." About thirty yards down the beach sat a shark, fin straight up in the air.

"If it washed up, shouldn't it be on its side?"

Marco didn't give an answer, because he didn't like the only one that came to mind.

The shark moved forward on the sand.

John took off his glasses and wiped them with the bottom of his shirt. "I must be seeing things." He put them back on.

Marco's mouth dried up. "It's not a shark," he whispered. "It's a *sharkodile*."

"A *what*?" John stepped forward.

"Don't!" Marco grabbed him and whispered, "It almost ate me and Sarah before!"

John shot him a look and then pushed Marco behind him. He spoke quietly. "We have to keep going. Maybe if we just—"

"We can't. If it sees us—" Marco froze as the sharkodile got up on its greenish reptilian legs. The beast turned, faced them, and paused.

"Is that for real?" asked John.

Marco held his breath.

Sharks had bad eyesight, right? There was no way it could see them that far down the—

The sharkodile charged, lightning on its four legs.

"Run!" Abandoning the silver container, Marco whipped back the way they had come, pumping both arms as he sprinted. As soon as he rounded the corner, he cut into the tree line.

John was right behind him. He yelled, "Where are you going?"

"If we hide, it might go on by." He slipped between two palm trees and ventured deeper into the brush, dropping behind a thick trunk. John hid behind a nearby one.

Marco gasped for air.

John set a finger to his lips.

Marco clapped a hand over his mouth.

The silver-and-green sharkodile passed them, going at a fast clip. As soon as the long, scaly tail slipped from view, John jumped up and motioned to Marco.

But Marco didn't move. He shook his head and leaned forward to peer through the foliage. He couldn't see the creature, but something told him that—

Silver and green flashed in front of him.

"Get up a tree!" he yelled at John.

The sharkodile thrust its snout through a bush. But its fin caught on the thorny branches, giving them a few precious seconds as the beast fought to free itself.

All around were only palm trees, impossible to climb. John found the lone monkey pod tree and made it up to a branch about six feet off the ground.

The sharkodile freed itself, pushing through the remainder of the bush.

"Marco! Run!" John leaned down, waving his arm. "I'll pull you up!"

But Marco was too far away. "I won't make it!"

A young palm tree was a few yards away, the nearest branch a good eight feet up. *Too high.* Still, Marco ran for it, reaching into his pocket and yanking out his knife. He flipped it open, sprinted, and leaped, jabbing the knife as far up the trunk as he could reach.

The knife hit true, deep enough to hold Marco as he tucked his legs and hung from one arm.

"It's coming!" yelled John.

Using his grip on the knife, Marco pulled himself up as much as he could, hoping he was far enough off the ground. His face was smashed against the rough trunk, the muscles in his arm and shoulder already beginning to burn from the strain of holding his entire body weight.

"It can't reach you!" called John. "You just have to hold on."

How was he going to do that?

With a grunt, he straddled the tree, tightening his legs as much as he could. He was able to switch hands and give his straining muscles a break.

But then he glanced down, right into the gaping red maw with jagged white teeth. He gasped. His arm tightened and his feet scrabbled against the trunk as he tried to get higher.

"Don't look down!"

Marco's feet slipped, but he kept going, trying to run up the palm tree even though it was impossible.

"Hold on!" John yelled. "It's leaving!"

Marco whirled in time to see the long green tail swish through the brush and disappear. He lost his hold and fell, landing on his backside with a grunt.

"Get up! Come on!" John waved his arm.

With wobbly legs, Marco got to his feet and ran over to John's tree. He thrust his weary arms up, and John pulled him to the lowest branch.

Exhausted and breathless, Marco slumped against the trunk.

"You okay?"

Marco said, "Well, *now* I am."

"What do you think we should do?" asked John.

Marco glanced at him. "What do *you* think we should do?"

John shrugged. "You've been around the island more than I have. And obviously seen things I haven't. I'd say you know a lot more than I do right now."

Marco thought a moment as he stared in the direction the creature had run. "I think maybe we wait a little while and then take another route back to the beach."

John didn't say anything at first. "Can we spare the time?"

Marco's words were firm. "We don't have a choice."

He waited for his stepfather to argue.

Instead, John touched Marco's cheek. "You've got a scrape."

"I'm fine." Marco rubbed his aching shoulder. "Could have been a whole lot worse." So much worse he didn't even want to think about it. He leaned back against the trunk, crossed his arms, and settled in to wait.

3

Sarah was hot and tired of walking, even though she was going extra slow to stall Fox.

Fox gave her a shove that sent her stumbling nearly to her knees.

She righted herself and put her hands on her hips. "I'm going as fast as I can!"

Fox took off his hat. "Well, I don't have all day." He wiped his sweaty face on his shirt, leaving a dark patch on the blue sleeve.

Sarah was lying of course; she could have moved faster, a *whole* lot faster. But she still hadn't come up with a plan. Dawdling was all she could think to do while she considered her options.

Should she stay on the beach or take the path into the woods?

Why hadn't she and Marco agreed on a plan before he left?

There had been no time, she told herself.

But that forced her to try and figure out what her stepbrother was thinking. Would he bring her dad the fast way, along the beach? Or would they be stealthy and take the inner route through the trees?

"Let's go, girly."

Sarah started walking.

Up ahead lay the path into the trees that she and Marco had taken the first time they'd discovered the face rock.

She had to make her choice. *Now.*

What was Marco thinking, where did he—?

Goose bumps rose on her arms. She had a funny feeling that Marco and her dad were close.

But which way?

Beach or trees?

Stay the course or choose the path?

Fox shoved her a little.

The path appeared.

Sarah made the call and pointed. "In there."

Fox gazed at the ocean for a moment, then back at the path. "Just remember. No funny business."

She scowled. "I want this over just as much as you do."

He held out a hand. "After you, girly."

Sarah stepped onto the dirt path and quickly entered the thicker part of the trees. The light grew dimmer as they progressed.

"This doesn't look familiar at all," said Fox.

None of it *would* look the same as when he'd been there. Sarah wondered whether he'd even believe the truth, that actual aliens—namely Leo and his grandfather—were responsible for the changes to the island: the larger volcano, all the trees, the strange creatures—

Sarah sucked in a quick breath. *The creatures.*

They were nearly at the exact spot where she and Marco had first seen the creature that appeared to be half rhinoceros, half unicorn. Maybe the rhinocorn was there, near them. As soon as she heard the chuffing, she could dive into the brush and get away, go find her dad. Because Fox would at least be startled, possibly even too freaked out to move.

Right?

She crossed her fingers and slowed her pace a little.

But by the time they reached the V in the path, they hadn't encountered anything. Sarah's shoulders slumped.

What did she do now?

The rock with the face lay on the path to the right. If she took Fox straight there, he'd know that this was the island, *his* island. And then he'd want the treasure.

Sarah decided to go left. Please let this be the best choice. She pointed. "That way."

The trees thickened. The path grew narrower. They were forced to move slower.

A shrill whistle cut the air.

"What was that?" asked Fox.

"Sounds like birds."

They were nearing the valley where she and Marco had seen all of those mysterious creatures. And Sarah still wasn't sure what to do once they arrived. Lost in thought, she grabbed a vine to move past, then let go. It slapped back into Fox's face.

"Watch it!"

A plan popped into Sarah's head. She slowed even more. When she was certain that Fox was right behind her, she took hold of a big clump of vines and pulled them out. She yanked tighter and tighter, until they wouldn't budge anymore.

She let go.

They snapped right into Fox's face.

"Hey!"

Sarah ran as fast as she could, brushing branches and leaves out of her face. If her plan had any chance of succeeding, she had to be quick. At least Fox had left his gun with Miss Blackstone. She didn't have to worry about him shooting her. Not yet.

She moved as fast as she could, dodging tree trunks. Her left foot caught on an exposed root and she tripped, catching herself before she fell. She shoved her way through a thick clump of vines that scratched her face.

The bird sounds grew louder. A raucous squawk startled her.

Almost there.

Sarah gasped for air. The path grew lighter, the opening loomed ahead. She pushed away the memory of the last time she'd been at that spot. She had to concentrate, had to time it just right or—

The ground fell away.

With a shriek, she slid to a stop in the dirt and fell back onto her hands, panting. Her feet were inches away from the edge of the cliff. Below, the green valley spread out, bordered on three sides by rocky walls. Although she'd seen the vista before, if she'd had any breath left, the view would have taken it away.

Rustling came from behind her.

Fox.

Sarah scrambled to her feet and stood as close to the edge of the cliff as she dared. Her knees wobbled as she caught sight of the tree branch she'd become acquainted with only a day before.

A scowling, panting Fox bolted out of the brush. He reached for Sarah.

She froze. *Wait for it. . . .*

Fox's fingers brushed her shirt.

She leaned away at the last possible second.

His momentum carried him toward the edge.

Sarah gasped and stepped back.

Time seemed to stop.

"Whoa!" Fox's arms windmilled frantically. He was on the edge of the cliff.

He was going to fall. . . .

And then he would be—

Could she do it? Was she the kind of person who could just stand there and watch while he—?

No.

Sarah leaped, grabbed his shirt, and pulled.

It was just enough.

Fox caught his balance and staggered back, away from the edge. His sunglasses fell to the ground, and for a moment, he hunched over, gasping for air as he stared over the edge. Slowly his eyes shifted to Sarah.

He straightened up.

Before she could say a word, he grabbed her arm and dragged her to the cliff's edge.

"No!" she screeched.

His grip was so hard it hurt as he swung her around and backed her up to the edge.

Solid ground disappeared under the toe of her left foot. Bits of dirt trickled down the rock. "Please, don't. I didn't mean—"

"You were fine with *me* going over." Fox pushed again.

"I saved you!" Sarah's left foot felt only air as her right foot slid halfway off the edge. She tried to gain purchase on the edge, but couldn't do anything except push against the face of the cliff with her foot.

Fox shoved farther.

Sarah found herself nearly horizontal, staring up at the blue cloudless sky.

The man's hold on her one stretched-out arm was the only thing keeping her from falling.

"Are you going to take me to the face rock?"

Sarah felt like her arm was about to be wrenched out of the socket. She scrunched her eyes shut tight. "Yes!" she screamed.

"No more messing around?"

Tears squeezed out of her eyes as her head fell from side to side, unable to speak as her heart felt like it could thump its way out of her chest.

Fox shook her like a rag doll. "Well?"

"I'll take you there, I promise! Pleasejustletme-backup." She gulped. *"Please."*

Fox yanked her forward and let go.

Sarah sprawled in the dirt. She curled up, gasping. Her heart had not slowed down one bit.

Fox said nothing for a moment. Then he nudged her with a foot. "Let's go."

Sarah slowly rose. She wiped her eyes with the back of her hand and brushed the dirt off her skinned knees. Even more wary of Fox than before, she pointed at the path. "Back that way. It's at the V, the other path."

Fox gestured impatiently. "Ain't got all day." He stooped down and grabbed his sunglasses.

And Sarah knew, then, that she was out of ideas. Her only hope was that Marco and her dad would come up with a way to help her before Fox discovered the truth. She only hoped that she would last that long.

4

Marco shifted on the branch, stiff from sitting in the same position. "How much longer should we wait?"

John shrugged. "Maybe that thing isn't coming back."

"We could be here all day." And they couldn't afford to waste that much time. Marco felt his pocket for the small case Leo had given him. At least he hadn't lost *that*. He had to get the medicine back to his mom.

And what if the criminals had already come ashore? What if they had hurt any of the others?

There was no more time to wait.

Marco gripped the branch and swung down, hanging by his arms. He let go and landed on the ground.

John shook his head. "I think you should get back up here."

"We can't just sit here and wait anymore." Marco took a few steps toward the beach, which, hopefully, was empty.

John dropped to the ground behind him. "See anything?"

Marco set a finger to his lips as he tiptoed closer to the edge of the trees. The beach was clear, the waves peaceful and calm.

His gut clenched.

The sharkodile could be out there, underwater, waiting for them. And once they reached the sand, there would be nowhere to hide, no defense against it. Marco pointed back toward the trees. "There might be a trail through here."

"Do you know one?"

Marco shook his head.

"We can't spare the time to find one."

Marco sighed. The only rational path was the beach. He whispered, "We run on three."

"Okay."

Marco held up one finger. Then two. He steeled himself, held up three fingers, and sprinted. He hit the sand and heard John's steady runs-every-day-but-Sunday exhalations behind him. After a few steps, he glanced sideways at the water. Still peaceful.

He ran as fast as he could, as far as he could, unable even to take the time to look for the food he'd dropped. Finally, he panted so loud he could barely hear his step-father behind him. He slowed to a walk, unable to keep up that pace.

"Do you think"—John gasped—"there are any more of those?"

Marco glanced at the water and wished he'd asked Leo just how many—and what kind of—creatures they should be on the lookout for. He sped up.

After a while of running and walking, both of them were exhausted and thirsty. But Marco smiled and pointed. "I recognize that dune by the bend. Our beach is right around it." He glanced out at the lagoon. The end of the sailboat was just visible.

"The boat looks empty," said John.

"You think they're all on the beach?"

"I do."

Marco sighed and patted his pocket. Every second they hesitated was more time his mother did without the medicine. "What now?"

John rubbed his forehead. "We have to estimate where they are."

Marco pictured their camp. "Maybe up by the fire?"

"We need to figure this out before we just come walking around the corner."

"I know." Marco surveyed the tree line. "I'll go and look. You stay here."

"Should we both go?"

Marco shook his head. "It's better to split up. That way if one of us runs into trouble—"

"The other can go for help?"

Marco frowned.

That was the thing. There *was* no help. They had only themselves. He gazed out at the sailboat again. Or maybe not . . .

John raised his eyebrows and faced the sailboat. "You think I should swim out there? Call for help?"

Then Marco remembered the sharkodile and shook his head. "Too dangerous."

John gazed back down the beach the way they'd come. He sighed. "My family is worth the risk." He kicked off his shoes. "I'll have no way of letting you know I made it."

"You could have some kind of signal." Marco thought for a moment. "Red. Send something red up the sail. I'll watch for it."

"But you won't know if I've been able to call for help."

Marco sighed. "It will take hours for anyone to get here anyway. I've got to get Mom the medicine as soon as I can."

"You're right," said John. "I'll try to call for help and then come back to the beach."

Marco shook his head. "You should stay. That way, if things go wrong or if they try to leave without us—"

"I can't leave you all here."

Marco said, "Then *I'll* swim out there."

John's forehead furrowed. "No way. Too dangerous." He set a hand on Marco's head. "Let me go. Hopefully I can call for help. And if not, then at least I'll be the backup plan."

"Okay." Marco's stomach churned.

John walked down to the water and stood there a moment, staring at the waves.

Marco wanted to reassure him. But his voice shook a little as he said, "That thing is probably still back there, where we left it."

John managed a smile. "Better call Guinness. I'm about to set a world record for the front crawl in sharkodile-infested waters." He held out a fist.

Marco bumped it with his own. Then, before he could think twice about it, he stepped forward and wrapped his arms around his stepfather. "Be careful."

"You too." John's arms went around Marco and squeezed. "See you on the other side, big guy." He rubbed Marco's hair a couple of times. He stepped back, ran into the waves, and dove.

Marco watched John's fast, steady crawl for a moment and then ran up the beach toward the tree line. He stepped between two thick trunks, then glanced back at the water. His stepfather was a diminishing dot in the waves.

Marco inhaled deeply. The next step belonged to him.

He tried to move quietly through the foliage, unsure how close he was to anyone in their camp. There was no telling where he would emerge. After only a few yards, the trees thickened, making for tough going through hanging vines and branches. Gradually they grew sparser. He crouched near a palm tree. He still couldn't see anyone, so he simply listened.

A woman's voice.

"I'm so tired of this island."

Mom?

He grinned. She was fine, *so* fine she actually had the strength to complain—

"Three days, he said. Three days and we'd have the treasure. Well, it's been way more than three days!"

No. This wasn't his mom. This woman's voice was nasal.

"Do you think I want to be here? Do you think I like standing up to my ankles in this disgusting sand?"

Marco dropped to his belly and crawled forward until the only thing between him and the woman was a short, stumpy clump of green grasses. He had a good view through the thick blades. The woman was dressed all in white, her eyes hidden behind her sunglasses, her red lips pursed in annoyance. Marco's gaze dropped to the trigger of the gun looped around one manicured finger, the scrawny white dog in the crook of her other arm.

"We can end this all right now and go home."

A man's voice. But who?

Marco shifted a bit to his left, to the edge of the clump. He saw a tree trunk, two smaller hands and two bigger, all encircled with rope.

"It's my sailboat; just let me go and we'll get out of here."

Cash's grandpa? Had to be.

The man's fingers furiously worked at the knots, even as his voice remained calm. "Leave Fox here."

The woman pouted even more. "Not without my treasure."

"There's no treasure." Sarge sounded irritated. "We've looked at every island between here and home port."

"Fox says this is the island." The woman tried to stomp a gold-heeled foot, which simply sank into the sand. "Ugh." She lifted her foot and shook out the grains. "That girl knows the place."

Marco sank lower in his crouch. Did she mean Sarah?

"I'm thirsty."

That was Cash. So Sarah had to have gone with Fox. But where?

Sarge said, "Please, can you get us some water?"

The woman held out her hand with the gun. "Do I look like I have water?"

"There's some up by the fire," said Cash.

Someone moaned.

Marco shifted back to the other side, as far as he dared, in order to see out. A blanket lay a few feet from Sarge. And there was a familiar sandaled foot—

Mom.

She was right there! So close.

"Fine. I'll go get you some water." The woman pointed the gun at them. "But you'd better not do anything while I'm gone." She whirled and minced her way up the beach, heels sinking into the sand with every step.

Marco burst out and ran straight to his mom.

"Marco!" whispered Cash.

He set a finger to his lips.

"Untie us!"

"In a sec." He glanced behind to make sure the woman was still heading away from them, then reached into his pocket and pulled out the case. A small vial of pink liquid lay inside. Exactly how much did he trust Leo?

Did it matter? He had no choice.

Marco dropped the case. He opened the vial and cupped the back of his mom's neck. "Mom?"

She moaned. Her eyes fluttered.

"Please, you've got to drink this." He held it to her dry lips.

She opened them slightly.

He managed to pour the contents into her mouth. He made sure she swallowed and then laid her head back down. She made no further movements, and her eyes remained closed.

How long would it take?

"Son, can you get us loose?" Sarge spoke quietly but firmly.

Marco reached into his pocket for the knife.

The knife.

He'd left it stuck in the tree back on the beach.

He smashed a hand over his face. "Stupid."

The dog's yapping startled Marco.

"She's coming back!" said Cash.

The woman turned their way.

Marco slid behind the tree. "Where'd Sarah go?"

"With Fox," said Cash. "To the face rock."

Miss Blackstone set the dog down. The ugly thing began running full out for the tree. And Marco.

The dog stopped a foot shy of him and the bushes, yapping like crazy.

The woman called out, "Bentley! Stop that! Come to Mama now."

Marco slid back behind the grasses. "I'll be back as soon as I can!" He crawled and then got to his feet as soon as he reached the trees.

Marco began to run.

He had to get to Sarah, he had to get to the face rock, and he had to—

Something hit him right in the midsection.

"Oomph." He doubled over and fell to his knees. He lay there and gasped for air as he wondered exactly which bad guy he had missed.

5

Sarah tried to stop crying as she led Fox, backtracking where they'd just come. She was so mad at herself.

She should have let him fall off the edge.

After all, he was mean and wanted to hurt her family. That was reason enough to let him fall to his doom, right?

But maybe it wasn't that simple. She probably would have felt terrible about it afterward.

She sniffled and wiped her eyes. No matter. The moment was over, and she couldn't get it back.

"How much farther?" Fox sounded very winded.

Sarah pointed. "Up there, at the V in the path."

Except for the receding squawks and whistles and tweets, their walk was silent.

She had no plan. She had to take Fox to the face rock. There was no getting out of it.

Sarah led Fox to the path she'd tried to avoid, speeding up slightly on the incline. There the trees grew farther apart, and they soon stepped out into the open space.

Fox stared.

Straight in front of them was the rocky cliff with the two indentations that looked like eyes.

"Voilà." Sarah held out her hand with a flourish. "The face rock." She stepped a few feet back from him, darting glances around the area. Could she make a run for it?

Fox seemed to ignore her as he strode forward to the base of the face. "This is it!" He whirled around, a grin on his face. "You did it, girly. I had my doubts, but—" He hocked up a loogie and spit.

Sarah cringed and took another step back.

The ground rumbled under her feet.

She froze.

Fox's eyes narrowed. "Did you feel that?"

The ground continued to vibrate. A loud chuffing sent a chill up her spine.

"What was *that?*" Fox stared into the trees they'd just emerged from.

"I don't know." Sarah's hands trembled. She knew

exactly what that sound was and what was headed toward them. She backed closer to Fox, not wanting to clue him in to anything. She snuck a glance at the crack in the wall, the one she and Marco had slid through.

The chuffing grew louder.

Her heart raced.

"What the—!" said Fox.

Sarah stood her ground and watched the trees.

A glimpse of gray flashed among the branches.

The rhinocorn!

Sarah twirled, sprinting.

Fox yelled.

Sarah reached the crack and didn't look behind her. She slipped in, scraping her arms on the rough rock. She knew there was no way Fox could fit.

There she paused, listening over her ragged breaths.

Other than that first yell from Fox, she'd heard nothing.

Had the rhinocorn gotten him? Had Fox found a place to hide?

Sarah listened a moment more, then sidestepped to her right. The rock closed in. The tightening space squeezed her as she headed toward the light at the other end. Part of her wanted to panic. This had been so much better when Marco was there with her.

You can do this.

Sarah squeezed her body as tight as she could. Finally, she pushed out the rest of the way and emerged in the sunshine. She leaned over and rested her hands on her knees.

Made it.

"I would have appreciated a warning, girly."

Sarah shrieked and straightened up.

Fox stood there, arms crossed, sunglasses askew on his nose. He reached up and tried to straighten them, but they stayed that way. "Blast." He took them off and bent them a little one way, then replaced them on his face. They were still crooked, but Sarah didn't say so.

Her hands trembled.

Why couldn't she get rid of him? The rhinocorn should have been enough.

"Come on, you've got work to do."

Sarah frowned. "What work?"

Fox grabbed her arm and pulled.

She stumbled forward and took an extra-long step to regain her balance.

Fox marched her the long way around the rock so fast that she was forced to jog. He stopped under the face and pointed at the base. "I don't know why there's a tree over it now, but when I left this place two years ago, my treasure was sitting right there, covered up by sand."

Sarah said, "Doesn't look like it's there now."

"Well, we're gonna find out, aren't we? Start digging."

Sarah's mouth fell open a bit. "With what?"

"Your hands, sweetie." He lunged for her.

She jumped back. "Fine! I'll do it."

Fox patted a spot on the ground with his foot. "Right here."

Slowly she knelt. The ground was hard and hurt her already-stinging knees.

"Dig!"

Sarah blinked back tears as she scooped the dirt and pushed it away. She didn't want to dig up his stupid treasure, mainly because she knew it wasn't there. His treasure was in the cave with Leo.

Sarah knew she could quit at any time; she could make it easy on herself, give in, and take him there. She didn't know what would happen, but at least then she'd be done with him and his shoving and his yelling.

She kept scooping and pushing.

Where was her dad? Marco?

No. It didn't matter. They were depending on her.

She had drawn the short straw for sure, getting stuck with Fox, but she needed to be exactly where she was to keep him away from the treasure.

"All you're doing is sweeping that stuff around!"

Sarah scowled. "I'm doing the best I can."

"Start digging. Get in there."

Fox's toe nudged her leg.

"Stop it!" Sarah jumped to her feet and flung out her hands, sending dirt everywhere. "Stop being mean! Your stupid treasure isn't even here—" Sarah stopped. Oh no!

Fox took a step back and removed his sunglasses. His eyes narrowed.

Sarah dropped to her knees and began digging in earnest.

Fox grabbed her arm and yanked her up. "You know where my treasure is?"

Sarah stared at the ground and shook her head.

"Hey! Look at me?"

Sarah scrunched her eyes shut.

"Show me where it is." Fox set her down on the ground.

Sarah opened her eyes. "I don't know where it is," she whispered.

"You're lying. I don't like it when people lie to me."

Sarah had been digging all right. Only it was herself, right into a hole. "Fine. Someone else has it."

"Really." Fox held out a hand. "Well, let's see now. There's you." He popped up one finger. "And your stepmother." Another finger. "And the sailboat guy's granddaughter." A third finger. "Seems like I've accounted for everyone." He crossed his arms. "How 'bout you tell me just *who* I'm missing here."

Sarah said nothing.

"NOW!"

Sarah jumped. "The Curator!"

Fox frowned. "The what?"

Sarah spit out the words so fast they all blended as one: "Helivesinthecaveandhecameheretogetanimalsand yourtreasurebelongedtohispeoplefirstandgotstolenfrom atribeinafrica—"

"Africa." Fox rubbed his chin. "I brought that treasure all the way from Africa."

"You stole it."

"I bought it!"

Sarah shook her head. "Then you bought it from the thief! It doesn't belong to you."

"Listen here—" He took a step toward her.

She backed up.

"Take me there. Now."

Sarah wanted to tell him no. She didn't want him anywhere near that treasure, which happened to be the progenitor, the astonishing, one-of-a-kind device that duplicated things and belonged to Leo and his alien race.

There was no telling what Fox would do if he found it.

Fox crossed his arms. "Maybe you'd be more inclined if we went back to your stepmother and—"

"No!" She didn't know what he was going to say, but she didn't want him anywhere near Yvonna. Maybe Leo could help. If she got Fox to the cave, maybe Leo could immobilize him or freeze him or something.

She pointed. "We have to go that way, back toward the beach."

"If this is another lie, I swear, I'll—"

Sarah shook her head vigorously. "No, I'm telling the truth. I'll take you the fastest way I know."

"Fine. Lead the way."

Sarah set off toward the beach. As she walked, she halfway hoped that the sharkodile would show up. And that it would have a particular taste for creeps with ugly hats and crooked sunglasses and bad attitudes.

6

Marco's solar plexus had taken the brunt of the blow. He curled up, forehead to the ground, waiting for some oxygen to make its way into his lungs. Slowly his diaphragm relaxed and a gasp of air trickled in, and then another. He slowly sat up, tensing as he faced his attacker.

His mouth fell open.

"Sorry." Nacho stood there, brandishing his backpack in both hands, biting his lip. "Thought you were a bad guy."

Marco sprung up and grabbed him.

"I said I was sorry!" Nacho tried to pull away, only to find himself wrapped in a hug.

"I'm so glad to see you."

Nacho relaxed in Marco's arms. "You are?"

"Believe it or not." Marco let go. "Tell me what happened back at camp."

"Well, the bad guy came to shore."

"Fox?"

"Yeah. He tied Cash up and chased Ahab off and then he went out and brought back Sarge and that lady." Nacho scrunched up his nose. "I don't like her."

Marco smiled. "Me neither. What about Sarah?"

"She went with Fox. I tried to untie her and Cash, but the knots were too tight and—" His eyes filled with tears.

Marco set a hand on his head. "Hey, it's okay."

"I really wanted to help."

"I know." Marco scratched his chin. "We've got to help now."

"Did you get John free?"

"Yeah I did. Well, Leo did. John swam out to the boat to call for help."

Nacho grinned. "So we're getting saved?"

"Not sure. Maybe." Marco's gaze darted around the trees. "Look, we need to get farther away from camp."

"But we have to help them." Nacho frowned. "We can't leave Mom."

"I gave her some of Leo's medicine."

51

Nacho's eyes grew big. "Did it make her better?"

"I couldn't stay to find out."

"Oh." Nacho slumped. "Do you think it did?"

Although he had no idea, Marco said, "I'm sure it did."

"Where are we going?"

"Well, if Sarah took him to the face rock, I guess that's where we need to go." Marco frowned and tried to get his bearings. They could cut back out to the beach and take the path he and Sarah had taken to the face rock. Or he could fumble his way through the trees, a gamble, as he would simply be guessing.

"What was that?" asked Nacho.

Marco hadn't heard anything. "What was what—?"

A rustling in the underbrush sent a chill down his neck. "Come on," he whispered, and pulled Nacho closer to a tree. It wasn't enough to hide them; he could only hope they'd be passed by.

Through the greenery a few yards away, black fur flashed.

Marco's hands shook as he pushed his brother a few steps behind him.

The rustling grew closer.

"Marco?"

"Shhh!" He could think only of the black cat, the

one that attacked Leo's grandfather. If it came for them, he had no knife, no defense—

A black shape sprang from the trees.

"Aaaaaaahhhhhhhh!" Marco shot his hands up in front of his face and squeezed his eyes shut.

He was knocked to the ground. An enormous weight pounced on his chest and felt as if would crush his lungs.

This was it.

He was never going to make it off the island.

He was meeting the same end as Leo's grandfather. The cat was going to tear him—

Something warm and wet and slippery licked him from chin to forehead.

Marco opened his eyes a crack.

The huge pink tongue was attached to one panting and wriggling Newfoundland perched on top of him.

Marco relaxed and set a hand on Ahab's head. "Hey, boy."

"Ahab!" Nacho hugged the dog. "I'm so glad to see you." He grasped his collar and pulled him off Marco.

"Me too." Relieved, Marco lay back on the ground for a moment.

"Now there's three of us." Nacho hugged the dog again.

Marco sat up and scanned their surroundings, just

in case Ahab wasn't the only thing running around that part of the island. They were lucky, he knew. Odds were, it was but a matter of time before they encountered something a little less welcoming than Ahab. Even though it was dangerous, they needed to get to the face rock the most direct way. Which meant heading back to the beach.

"Let's go find Sarah." Marco directed Nacho, but took up the rear, wanting to make sure that nothing snuck behind them. When they reached the beach, Marco took hold of Nacho's arm. "Hold on a sec."

The beach appeared empty. Still . . . "Nacho, we're going to run for a bit, okay?"

His brother frowned. "I'm tired of walking."

Marco really didn't want to explain that their life might be in danger if they took their time. "I don't want to be exposed that long."

"Why?" Nacho's eyes narrowed. "What's out there?"

"Nothing. But if Fox is watching for us, then—"

"Oh," said Nacho. "I get it. We need to sneak up on them."

Marco nodded. "Exactly." He stepped onto the sand in the direction they needed to go. "Ready to run?"

"Yes." Nacho stepped in front of Marco and then

turned back. "Do you think . . . ?" His words trailed off and his eyes grew huge. His mouth fell open.

Marco's chest tightened. Oh no, the sharkodile. If it had already seen them, there was no escape; they couldn't run fast enough—

BOOM!

Ahab barked.

Marco whirled around.

The sky dripped red, the streaks began to swirl together, and they formed a crimson orb like before.

"Run!" Marco pushed his brother forward and they sprinted down the sand, Ahab beside them. The thick sand was too challenging; Marco's already-weary legs were burning. He knew Nacho couldn't keep up that pace. Still running, he pulled on Nacho's elbow, steering him to the hard-packed sand closer to the water.

Marco shot a glance backward.

The red orb hurtled toward them.

"Faster!" Marco caught sight of the opening in the trees, the path. He gasped, "Almost there!"

Nacho stumbled and pitched forward, arms out to break his fall.

Marco grabbed his brother by the backpack, yanking him upright. Their legs churned. They reached the thick sand and headed up toward the tree line. "There! Run!" Marco nearly shoved his brother into the trees.

Ahab was right on their heels, too close, and tripped them.

Boys and dog tumbled in a heap in the shade of the trees.

A second later, the red ball flashed by.

Marco lay there, pulse pounding in his ears.

Ahab panted next to him.

Nacho rolled over onto his back, gasping. "That . . . wasn't . . . good."

"Well, of course it wasn't." Marco sat up. "We almost didn't make it."

Nacho panted a bit. "No, I mean that thing." He rolled over and got up on his knees. "It was a message for Leo."

Marco wiped his sweaty face on the shoulder of his shirt. "So?"

"Don't you get it?" Nacho leaned forward. "Leo is on a countdown. And he's running out of time."

7

The full brunt of the hot sun beat down on Sarah as she trudged along the beach beside Fox. They heard the *boom* and ran into the trees moments before the orb streaked by.

The whole thing left the man looking freaked out and exhausted.

Sarah wondered what would happen if she just ran as fast as she could away from him. But if she did that and she lost him, Fox would probably be able to make his way back to their camp. And she didn't want him there alone with Yvonna and Cash and Nacho and a gun.

Her dad and Marco needed to get there first.

As she walked along, Sarah at least knew enough to be wary. She scanned the waves for a fin. If the sharkodile showed up, she didn't have to outrun *it*. She just had to outrun Fox.

Sarah nearly smiled.

Fox becoming a snack for that thing wouldn't be her fault at all.

"Here." Fox pushed a warm bottle of water against Sarah's arm.

She'd forgotten they had some and guzzled half the bottle, before gasping.

"How much farther?" Fox finished the other bottle of water.

Sarah wasn't sure. She remembered that she and Marco had run from the sharkodile and had seen the entrance to the cave not long after. They had to be close. "Soon. I think."

Fox stopped. "You *think*?"

Sarah's free hand became a fist. "I've only been there once! I don't remember *specifics*. I'll get us there when I get us there." She cringed, expecting Fox to yell.

Instead, he simply sighed. "Fine. But it better be soon." He wiped his red, sweaty forehead with his ugly hat.

Sarah finished the rest of the water. She carried the bottle for a little ways before casually letting it go. She didn't condone littering. But maybe someone looking for her would see it and figure out she'd come this way. Besides, she still held out the tiniest bit of hope that they might run into her dad and Marco at any time.

There were a few rocks on the beach. Sarah pictured Marco picking one up to ward off the sharkodile. They were getting close.

Sarah studied the tree line and tried to remember if the entrance to the cave was easy to spot, or if she had to be standing a certain way. Then, suddenly, the dark, yawning mouth of the cave appeared. "There." She pointed.

A slow grin spread across Fox's face. "Well, lookie there. A cave." He held out a hand. "After you."

Sarah bit her lip. At least this time she knew what to expect. Her first step through the mouth was once again followed by a slight ripple through her body.

Fox followed her. "Hey! Did you feel that?"

Sarah raised her eyebrows, trying to look as innocent as possible. "What?"

"Never mind." Fox frowned. "It's really dark."

"Well, it *is* a cave." She took a step.

"Wait!"

She faced him. "Are you afraid?"

"No, I'm not *afraid*." The last word was in baby talk. But Fox looked a little shaken.

Sarah had to admit the thought of moving forward into the blackness—even though she knew the way lightened after only about twenty yards—made her uneasy. But this path was the only way she knew for sure to get to Leo. She reassured Fox, and herself. "It's only dark for a little ways."

"Fine. No funny business."

Sarah set one hand against the rough wall and slid it along as she descended into the darkness. She didn't try to reach out for the left side, sticking to the right.

"You there?" Fox's voice trembled a bit.

Was he afraid of enclosed spaces? Or darkness?

"Yes." Sarah felt a little better. She was nervous, but not downright terrified. "Right here. Just keep moving. It'll get light. . . ." Even as she said the words, a faint glow ahead grew brighter and brighter, making it easier to see.

A moment later, Sarah stepped out into the vast cavern, lit as bright as day.

Fox whistled. "This was definitely not here before."

Sarah shivered at the chill. The white modules were there, as before, and she headed down the center row.

A pure white butterfly, with wide black tips on its wings, fluttered by. Sarah watched it ascend, just in time for a bird to whoosh by. "Whoa!" She ducked. Expecting another mutant, she whirled around to look for four wings or teeth or something equally freaky.

The bird circled.

Beneath a bluish-gray head, the neck bore some iridescent feathers, ranging from bright violet to golden green, and the breast was various shades of pink. The upper back and both wings were a pale gray, and the tail had white outer edges with blackish spots.

The bird was beautiful. And perfectly normal.

Another white butterfly, identical to the other, flew by, followed by two bright blue ones with white spots on their wings.

They *all* seemed to be normal.

Had Leo figured out how to use the progenitor and replicate the creatures he needed?

"What's in these things?" Fox paused in front of one of the frosted-over modules.

Sarah tore her gaze away from the flying creatures. "Clear the frost and see."

Fox frowned. "You've been here before?"

"Yes."

"And you saw these things before."

"Definitely."

"And you say my treasure is here?"

She pointed to the very end of the row. "Probably down there."

Fox brushed past her, striding along.

She jogged to keep up, slowing only when she reached the end, and the module where she'd last seen her father. The door was closed, as before.

She walked slower and slower as she got closer and closer.

What if her dad was still in it? What if Leo had lied and hadn't let him out? Worse, what if he'd frozen Marco too?

She stepped up to the window, but didn't look. "Please be empty, please be empty. . . ." She raised her gaze. The module was empty.

Her dad was free.

Then where was he?

Sarah leaned her forehead against the cool glass.

Why hadn't he found her yet? Was he even *looking* for her?

"Don't, Sarah," she whispered. Stop being a baby.

Her dad was probably doing something, right that minute, to get them all rescued. Maybe Marco was too.

And she had to do her part. Unfortunately, that part was here, with Fox, in the cave.

"What the—?"

Sarah jumped at Fox's outburst.

A shiny white divider blocked the way at the far end of the cavern. A flash of white light came from behind it.

"That wasn't there before." She added, "I swear."

Fox froze a few steps in front of Sarah.

Sarah shielded her eyes. That light was the same as the light that came from the trunk when Leo had opened it at the beach. He *had* to have figured out the progenitor.

The light gradually began to fade and then disappeared altogether.

Suddenly, from around the edge of the divider, padded a muscular, light brown animal the size of a large dog. Chocolate stripes ran down the rear half of its back. With small ears perked upright and a twitching, shiny black nose at the end of a long muzzle, the creature studied them with bright, dark eyes. Its long, thin, nearly hairless tail slowly swept from side to side.

Sarah knew she should have been afraid. But instead, she felt something else.

"What *is* that?" whispered Fox.

Sarah sensed that this animal wasn't a mutant. Like

the bird and the butterflies, something about this one seemed too . . . real.

With a squeak, the creature yawned, revealing sharp, white teeth.

What *was* that thing?

She'd been to the San Diego Zoo so many times and had seen *all* the animals. Although she wouldn't admit it to Marco and Nacho, she'd also watched a fair amount of shows on Animal Planet.

But she hadn't seen any shows featuring this one.

The animal began to pace back and forth, nails clicking softly on the floor of the cavern.

Fox stepped back, cowering behind Sarah. "Is it going to attack?"

Sarah ignored him. The animal's pacing mesmerized her.

Back and forth. Back and forth.

So familiar.

She had totally seen an animal like this before, moving that same way.

If not in person at a zoo and not on television, then where? Other than that, there was only the web—

The visual came to her, of the short black-and-white clip on the internet.

A zoo in Hobart, Australia.

The 1930s.

An animal . . .

. . . in a stark concrete-and-metal cage.

Pacing.

Alone.

Truly alone.

The last of its kind.

Goose bumps sprouted on her arms as she realized no one had seen this animal in decades.

"But that's . . . impossible."

Sarah dropped to her knees. "You're supposed to be extinct."

8

Marco put both hands on top of his head. What was he supposed to do?

Run around hunting for his stepsister?

Or go help an alien that had given him medicine for his mom?

Even though he still didn't know whether the vial had worked, he had the feeling it was legit. And he had promised he would return to help Leo, whose time appeared to be running out.

"New plan."

Nacho stroked Ahab's head. "Aren't we going to find Sarah?"

"Maybe Sarah is leading Fox to Leo's cave."

"Why would she do that? He wanted to see the face rock."

"But maybe she went there instead."

"Maybe she didn't."

Marco rolled his eyes. "Listen, it's been a while since they left, right?"

"Quite a while," said Nacho.

"So I think there's a chance they could be at the cave already. Sarah can take care of herself." When they'd started on the trip back in California, he never would have thought such a thing. But since they'd been on the island, it was clear he'd misjudged her. She was much tougher than he'd first thought. Smarter too. And he did think there was a chance she was, indeed, leading Fox to the cave.

"What if she can't?" Nacho adjusted his backpack.

"Nacho!" Marco groaned. "We need to go to the cave."

"You go."

"Oh, come *on*." What was with his little brother? Why wasn't he just going along with him?

"You didn't see him," said Nacho.

"See who?" asked Marco.

"That guy. Fox. He is *mean*. I don't like Sarah being alone with him. You shouldn't either."

"Well, of course I don't—"

Nacho crossed his arms. "We should be going to the face rock to help her. Or maybe you don't care."

Marco slapped his hands on his thighs. "Of course I care. But we have to go to the cave!"

"Fine. You go." Nacho hitched up his backpack.

Ahab whined.

"What's wrong?"

The dog whined again and then panted.

Marco said, "I think he's thirsty."

Nacho sighed, set his backpack on the ground, and unzipped it. Several bottles of water lay inside.

"Nice." Marco opened one up and took a big swig.

"Hey. What about the dog?" Nacho knelt down and cupped his hands. "Okay, pour some water in. See if he'll drink it."

Marco poured some water into Nacho's grimy hands. "Here, boy!"

Ahab was more thirsty than particular, and lapped up the water in no time. Marco poured more, continuing until the bottle was empty. Ahab sat back on his haunches, his tail thumping the dirt. Then, with a bark, he bounded into the trees.

Nacho wiped his slimy hands on his shorts and grabbed the backpack.

"Nacho! Where you going?"

"To get my sister."

"Are you serious?"

"Yes!" He took a few steps.

Marco frowned. "And she's not your sister! She's your *step*sister."

Nacho faced him and threw his arms out to the sides. "After all this? Hanging on to the whole *step* thing seems pretty stupid."

Marco stared at his little brother, his gaze drifting over the wrinkled, smeared clothes and the smudges of dirt on his face. Before this trip, Nacho wouldn't even go outside without bathing in hand sanitizer, let alone let a *dog* drink from his hands.

In a few short days, Nacho had become a different person. A stronger person. And, despite his quirks and annoyances, he was rational. Maybe the most rational person Marco knew. He sighed. "Fine. We'll go to the face rock. But we've got to move fast. Okay?"

Nacho grinned. "We will."

They pushed through the foliage and vines, following the dog. Marco hoped Ahab was headed toward the path, otherwise this would take them forever.

Nacho said, "Sarah didn't have to do it."

"Huh?" Marco slapped a vine out of his way.

"I saw her. Fox was taking Cash and Mom to the boat and Sarah stopped him."

Marco paused. "How did she do that?"

Nacho's face popped out between the slim gray trunks of two trees. "That's when she told him about the rock with the face. Like she knew that would get him to stay."

Marco took a step back. No one had asked Sarah to do that and put her own life in danger. But if she hadn't, his mom could be anywhere by now. And she wouldn't have taken the medicine. Sarah's quick thinking might have saved his mom's life.

Up ahead, the dog barked.

"Marco! Hurry." Nacho slipped through several low-hanging branches and disappeared.

"Wait!" A branch snagged Marco's shirt. He yanked himself loose and fought his way through a stubborn clump of vines. He emerged onto the path he and Sarah had been on before. The V was straight in front of them.

Ahab wagged his tail.

"Good boy." Marco patted his head.

Nacho asked, "Which way now?"

Marco pointed at the path to the right.

Ahab barked and took a few steps along the trail

that headed to the beach and water. He turned to look at the boys.

"No, Ahab, this way." Marco stepped onto the right path and slapped his hand on his thigh. "Come on."

Ahab barked again, moving farther away.

Nacho said, "I think he wants us to go that way."

Marco gestured. "But the face rock is *this* way."

"I think we should follow Ahab."

Marco sighed. "Now you're letting the *dog* decide?"

Ahab took off running and Nacho went after him.

Marco had one choice. He followed.

The dog moved fast. Remarkably, so did his little brother. Marco was out of breath by the time they reached the beach.

Ahab barked. Then he took a few steps in the direction of Leo's cave.

Marco shrugged. "Let's follow him."

Ahab trotted down the sand, the boys on his heels.

As they moved along, Marco scanned the water, eyes peeled. But, for the moment, the waves remained fin free.

"Hey!" Nacho jogged ahead a bit and snatched something up. He held out a water bottle. "Maybe it was Sarah's?"

Marco's gaze dropped. Two clear sets of footprints

sunk into the sand, one an adult's, one much smaller. "Who else could it be?"

Nacho said, "Sarah's heading to the cave."

Marco's eyes locked with his brother's. "Let's go get her."

9

Sarah stared at the animal in front of her, wondering if she should even believe her eyes.

"What's that?" Fox pointed.

From behind the partition came Leo in his natural state, gills and all, white weapon tube in his hand. He crouched as soon as he saw them.

Sarah got to her feet. "Oh, that's just Leo."

"What is he?"

"An alien."

Just then, the animal whirled toward the alien boy, who raised the tube.

"No!" cried Sarah.

Immediately the animal tried to fight off the white net. But the shrinking net quickly immobilized the creature, which ceased to struggle and fell over on one side.

Sarah ran over. "Why did you do that?" She dropped to her knees beside the creature and set a hand on its heaving side. "Is it hurt?"

"No, of course not," said Leo.

Sarah studied the creature, whose dark, expressive eyes gazed up at her. "Is this what I think it is?"

"Tasmanian tiger," said Leo.

"Wait, so this means you did it? You figured out how to use the progenitor?"

Leo grinned. "I've been busy." He dropped his head back and stared up at the butterflies. "Some I still have to catch, though."

Sarah touched a patch of the tiger's fur that stuck out of the netting. "I'm touching an animal no one has touched since . . . who knows when?" She stayed there a moment, feeling the energy of the creature.

The bird flew overhead.

"And what's that?"

"Passenger pigeon."

"It's beautiful." She rubbed the tiger once more. "You have to let it go." Sarah jumped to her feet. "It belongs in the wild."

Fox said, "No way. That belongs in a zoo. You know how much people would pay to see it?"

Leo asked Fox, "Who are you?"

Fox smiled his smarmy smile. "*What* are you?"

Sarah wanted to tell Leo about Fox, tell him he was bad, but before she had a chance, the boy asked Sarah, "Do you know what would happen if we released this one Tasmanian tiger back into its natural habitat? Do you?"

Sarah's thoughts whirled. "Yes. It would be free."

"Would it? For how long?" Leo's voice was soft. He wasn't arguing. The passenger pigeon winged by again, and then the butterflies. "There's more than one reason why they all went extinct." He side-eyed Fox. "And those reasons have not gone away."

Tears welled up in Sarah's eyes. "I know, but . . . the tiger should be free. Not have to live in a cage." Fox stepped up to get a closer look at the tiger.

Leo set a webbed hand on Sarah's arm. "Come here." He led her down the row of modules, to one that was just beginning to frost over. "Look."

Sarah pressed her face to the glass.

A Tasmanian tiger stood inside, eyes bright, slight mist around the snout. "Another one?"

"This is the mate. When we get to my planet, we will set them free. And no one will hurt them. Ever."

Sarah faced him. "You promise?"

Leo smiled. "Yes. I promise." He lifted an arm and gestured down the row. "That's why we're doing all of this. For my people and our planet, yes." He pointed at the module. "But for them too."

"But what if . . ." Sarah sniffled. "What if you make it back to your planet and . . ."

Leo's forehead creased. "And what?"

"What if it's not how you thought it would be?"

Leo's shoulders slumped. He breathed out, long and hard.

"What if, all this time, you've been trying so hard to get to a place that . . . that you can't return to?" Sarah felt bad saying it aloud. But it was true, wasn't it? His Cry of the Ancients, the collection of animals—they were all because of a place he had never seen or been to. Neither had any of his people on the ship.

Leo smiled the tiniest bit. *"Hiraeth."*

"What?"

"It's a word on your planet that means being homesick for a place that you can't return to. Or maybe, a place that never even was."

Sarah stared at the Tasmanian tiger and felt a lump in her throat. The tiger couldn't go back.

She thought about her mom, how much she missed her. Oh, how Sarah wished she could return to her embrace, be in that place of safety and love.

Tears welled up.

Was it the same, in a way?

Leo longing for his world . . .

The Tasmanian tiger, pacing in that long-ago cage in the Hobart Zoo, longing for his . . .

And Sarah, herself. She could never return to her mother's arms; they were lost for good, but . . .

Leo still had a chance.

Her gaze swept down the closest modules that contained animals gone from the earth forever, never to return. The passenger pigeon overhead, the butterflies . . .

They *all* still had a chance.

She couldn't stand in the way. She glanced back at the immobilized tiger and gasped. "Where's Fox?" Sarah stepped closer to Leo and spoke softly. "He stole a sailboat from Cash's grandpa. He's looking for the trunk. *Your* trunk."

Leo's grip on the white tube tightened. "Why?"

"He's the one who stole it from the tribe. Or else got

it from the ones who stole it." Sarah shook her head. "It doesn't matter."

"He can't have it," growled Leo. "I won't let him." He glanced at the tiger. "I've got to get him in a module. Can you help me?"

"Okay."

Together they gently dragged the Tasmanian tiger across the smooth floor and inside an empty module.

"Wait, just one second?" Sarah crouched beside the creature and set her hand on its head. A tear ran down her cheek.

"Everything okay?"

"Yeah." She straightened up and backed out of the module.

Leo twisted the end of the tube. A puff of steam came out and dissolved the net. Leo quickly shut the door as the animal got to its feet. He handed Sarah the tube and pressed the keypad.

Slowly mist filled the module, starting the stasis process.

Sarah leaned the tube against the module and pressed both hands on the glass.

Leo stood beside her, watching too.

Within moments, the tiger was still and silent.

Sarah whispered, "Sweet dreams."

"Well, isn't this touching?"

Sarah gasped.

Fox stood ten feet away, evil grin on his face, the white tube now firmly gripped in his hands and aimed straight at Leo. "Now, how 'bout somebody show me where my treasure is?"

10

Marco, Nacho, and Ahab sped along the beach. When they needed a break, they walked until they could run once more. During one rest, Nacho pulled another two bottles of water from his backpack. As Marco cranked one open, Nacho said, "These are the last ones."

Marco glanced down at Ahab, whose pink tongue seemed to hang halfway to the ground. "Let's give him some first."

"Good idea." Nacho cupped his hands.

Ahab lapped up the water. Then he licked Nacho's hands as clean as possible, minus the dog slobber. Then Nacho and Marco shared the one remaining bottle. Nacho put the empties in his backpack and zipped it.

"Want me to carry it?" asked Marco.

"I got it." Nacho looped it over a shoulder. "It's a lot lighter now." He wiped the sweat off his forehead. "How much farther?"

Marco took a few steps down the beach and scrutinized the tree line. He pointed. "It's there. The cave is right there."

Nacho took hold of Ahab's collar. "Do we just go in?"

"I guess." Marco glanced at the backpack. "Got a flashlight in there?"

Nacho shook his head. "But I have this from my last camping trip with the Eco-Scouts." He pulled out a package of green glow sticks.

Marco frowned. "But you said you felt sick. Mom let you stay home."

Nacho opened the package. "That's why I've still got them." He snapped two glow sticks and handed one to Marco.

"Thanks." He led the way to the mouth of the cave. "So when we go through, you might feel like a . . ."

"A what?" Nacho's forehead wrinkled.

"A tingle? Like a little electric shock." Marco hoped it was as *little* as he remembered. He stepped through. The buzz spread out through his body, almost over as soon as it started.

Ahab came next. He barked and jumped like he'd been bit.

"You're okay, boy." Marco gripped his collar.

Nacho hesitated. "Does it hurt?"

"No! Just come on."

Nacho scrunched his eyes shut and leaped through. "Oh! That was weird."

Marco sighed and held up his glow stick. "Ready? It's dark up ahead."

"Yeah." Nacho adjusted his backpack and brandished his glow stick. "Ready."

Marco took a few steps. "Let's be quiet, okay? We don't know what's happening in there."

"Got it."

Ahab's panting and the shuffling of their footsteps along the rocky bottom echoed slightly. The walls, glowing green from the glow sticks, closed in.

Marco stopped. He covered his glow stick with his hand and whispered, "It's getting lighter ahead. We're almost there." He set his glow stick on the ground, then tightened his hold on Ahab's collar and put a finger on his lips.

Nacho stuck up a thumb.

Marco stepped as lightly as he could the rest of the way, until he was on the verge of the massive cavern.

The place was lit as brightly as always, the white modules glaring after the dimness of the passage.

He ran, pulling Ahab over to the nearest row of modules. When Nacho was beside him, Marco leaned out and tried to see if anyone was farther down.

The place seemed deserted. But his gut told him the opposite.

"Hold Ahab and stay here," he whispered.

"But I want to go with you."

Marco sighed. "I want to do a quick scout, okay? As soon as it's safe, you can come out."

"Fine." Nacho grabbed ahold of the dog's collar and knelt beside him. "We have to stay here, boy."

Ahab licked his face.

Marco paused for a deep breath, then stepped out and ran halfway down the row. He ducked into a gap between two modules and peeked out. Still no movement from the other end of the space.

Wouldn't Leo be there, trying to fill the modules?

Maybe the progenitor had failed.

But where was Sarah? Had she and Fox made it to the cave?

Marco ran farther along the row until he found another gap big enough to hide in.

Then he heard the murmur of voices.

One was deep, a man's for sure. And the higher-pitched ones: Sarah's, maybe? Leo's?

A movement overhead caught Marco's eye.

A bird. A beautiful gray bird.

With only two wings.

Not a freak.

It worked. The progenitor worked!

Marco slipped out of his hiding spot and crouched, quietly moving down the aisle, his arm brushing the modules as he passed by.

At the end of the row, he knelt on one knee and leaned out far enough to see with one eye. Next to some kind of divider about ten yards away stood a man in a blue shirt and dirty cargo shorts and a dumb-looking Panama hat. Fox, obviously. And he gripped a white tube in his hands.

Marco's stomach was in knots.

"Careful, now. Careful," said Fox.

Leo and Sarah came into view, lugging the trunk.

"Oh no," whispered Marco.

"I said *careful*. That's my treasure."

Marco's heart raced.

Fox was trying to steal the progenitor back.

Sarah and Leo set the trunk down.

"Oh, hold on, now. This loot is going all the way back to the beach and my boat."

"It's not your boat." Sarah sounded out of breath. "It belongs to Sarge."

Fox laughed and held up the tube. "I've seen what this thing can do. Once we get back to the beach, you'll all be wrapped up like little presents. And I'll be on my way with *my* treasure. And my new cash cow."

Sarah frowned. "What are you talking about?"

Fox tapped the tube on the chest. "Antiquities are one thing." His gaze slid sideways to Leo. "Aliens are totally another. I'll never have to work again."

Marco clamped a hand over his mouth. Would Fox really take Leo?

Sarah crossed her arms. "I don't see any aliens."

Fox scowled. "What do you call Fish Boy here?"

Sarah shrugged. "I just see a boy. Right, Leo?"

Leo met Sarah's gaze. His gills and webbed hands disappeared. "Right."

Marco grinned.

"Hey!" Fox looked from one to the other. "What happened?"

"I told you," said Sarah. "He's just a boy."

Marco pulled back and leaned against the module,

out of sight once more. Maybe now Fox would forget about Leo. But they couldn't be allowed to leave the cave, especially not with the trunk. If Leo had truly determined how to use the progenitor, then he had to stay and finish his work before his time ran out.

Somehow Marco had to get that tube away from Fox.

"Let's go." Fox waved his free arm. "Come on, come on, I don't have all day."

With a groan, Sarah picked up her end of the trunk as Leo hefted his.

Marco made a fist and released it. He did it again as he tried to figure out what to do. He could wait there, let them walk by, and then tackle Fox. Granted, the man was bigger than he was, but Marco had the advantage of surprise, not to mention some martial arts skills. It might be enough to distract Fox and give the others a chance to help disarm him.

Leo and Sarah neared his hiding spot.

Marco sucked in a breath and tried to shrink into the slim space even more.

They were almost there, Fox right behind them.

Marco held his breath. Wait for it . . . wait.

"Woof! Woof!"

The end of the trunk dropped out of Sarah's hands as Ahab bounded into view and hopped up on her.

"Ahab, no!" Marco covered his mouth, but too late.

Fox swung the tube in his direction and fired.

Marco shut his eyes and hoped it wouldn't hurt.

Sarah screamed, "No!"

Marco's eyes shot open.

Ahab lay in front of him, enmeshed in the white net, his struggles already slowing. The dog whined.

Fox took aim at Marco again.

"Nooooooo!" With a grunt, Nacho ran across the space and rammed the man with all his might. Fox went down on one knee, and Nacho slipped and fell.

The tube skittered across the floor, and Marco dove for it.

Before Nacho could get back up, Fox grabbed him, his elbow bending around the boy's throat.

Marco hopped up and aimed the weapon at Fox. "Let him go!"

Fox stood up, shielding himself with a flailing Nacho. "Go ahead and shoot," Fox sneered. "You'll only get him."

Leo dropped his end of the trunk and stood by Sarah. He told Marco, "Release Ahab."

Marco twisted the end and pointed the tube at Ahab. Steam came out, dissolving the web. Seconds later Ahab got up and shook himself, his thick black fur rippling. He barked at the man.

Fox tightened his grip on Nacho.

"Let him go!" cried Sarah.

Nacho stopped kicking. His fingers scraped at Fox's arm, trying to loosen the stranglehold. His eyes bulged.

Marco aimed. Could he get a clear shot? What if he shot both of them? Then Fox could release Nacho and—

"I said, LET MY BROTHER GO!" Sarah ran over and kicked Fox in the shin.

Fox cried out in pain and nearly dropped Nacho before he regained his grip.

Ahab barked and moved closer.

"Keep that dog away from me!" yelled Fox.

Sarah kicked him again. "Let him go!"

Leo joined her and kicked Fox's other leg.

Grunting, Fox tried to back away with Nacho, but tripped over the boy's backpack and fell to the floor. Nacho scrambled away, clutching his throat and coughing.

Immediately Ahab put one paw on Fox's chest and growled.

"Get him off!" Fox threw up his hands and cowered. "Get him off!"

"No way," said Sarah. "Good boy, Ahab."

Marco tossed the tube to Leo and then pulled Nacho to his feet. "You okay?"

"I think so."

The ground shook underneath their feet.

Leo's face grew pale.

"Another red ball?" asked Marco.

Leo nodded. "There will only be two more after this one. I don't have much time."

"What can we do?" asked Sarah.

"I have to catch the butterflies and that bird." His eyes drifted to the modules at the end of the row that had contained Nacho, John, and Ahab. "And—"

"You have to refill those," said Marco.

Sarah frowned at Leo. "What's he talking about? *Refill* them? With *what*?"

"More like, with *whom*," muttered Marco.

Sarah gasped as she understood. "No! You're not putting them back in there."

Leo glared at Marco and raised the tube. "We made a deal. You got your end of it."

"What deal?" Sarah put her hands on her hips.

Nacho crossed his arms. "Yeah. What deal?"

Marco's mind raced. He *had* promised Leo. John and Nacho and Ahab had been let out of those modules. And now they needed to be replaced before Leo could leave.

Marco watched Fox for a moment. "So. Leo." He smiled. "Do they have to be the same humans?"

Sarah's eyes widened. Then she grinned. "Or the same dog?"

Leo shook his head.

"Somebody grab Ahab," said Marco.

Sarah took hold of his collar.

Marco stepped closer to Fox and aimed. "On three, pull him off."

Fox sputtered, "Hey, hold on there."

"One," said Marco.

The man held out his palms toward Marco. "We can split the treasure! Fifty–fifty!"

"Two."

Fox started to sit up. "Okay, okay! Sixty–forty! Seventy–thirty! There's enough for everyone."

"Three!"

Sarah pulled Ahab away as Marco fired.

Encased in the shrinking white net, Fox was soon nothing but a moaning white lump on the floor.

"Well, there's one down." Marco grinned. "And I'm pretty sure I know where we can get the other two."

11

Sarah helped the others drag Fox to the same module that had housed her father.

Marco said, "Lift on three!"

Leo opened the door of the module, and Sarah, Marco, and Nacho tilted the man inside. They deposited him on the floor, then backed out.

Leo told Marco, "Get ready to release him." Then he placed his webbed fingers over the keypad. "Now."

As soon as Marco twisted the tube, the netting began to dissolve. Fox struggled free of the remaining white strands.

Leo shut the door. He morphed back into his alien self and touched the panel with one webbed hand.

The mist began to rise in the module.

"Hey!" Fox pounded on the glass. "Let me out!" His eyes narrowed and he held up a fist. "I'll get you for this! I'll—"

And, just like that, he was stiff and still.

Sarah sighed with relief.

No more yelling. No more shoves or pushes or sneers.

She didn't feel badly about Fox, not at all.

Leo said, "We need to catch the butterflies and the passenger pigeon."

"What did you say?" asked Nacho.

"There." Sarah pointed out the bird overhead.

Nacho's mouth fell open.

Leo took the tube from Marco and aimed at the bird.

"Wait!" Sarah set a hand on his arm. "You can't just shoot it when it's flying."

"How do you think I caught his mate? Although it took me a while. They already built a nest in the corner." Leo took aim. "Get ready to catch it."

Marco and Nacho held out their arms and stared upward. Sarah did the same, shuffling around as she tried to get directly under the bird.

"Ready?" called Leo.

"Not yet!" yelled Sarah.

"Now!" The shot was true, white shrouding the

passenger pigeon, which stiffened and dropped from midair.

Marco elbowed Sarah out of the way.

"Watch it!" she called.

The bird landed in his arms, where he cradled it.

"Hold it out." Leo twisted the tube.

The net slowly dissolved.

Marco held the quivering bird in his hands, its bright eyes blinking.

"You're okay." Sarah stroked a wing with her fingertips.

Nacho touched it and whispered, "He's so soft."

"You know it's a male?" asked Sarah.

"He *would*. He did a huge diorama for his extinct-animal badge in Eco-Scouts." Marco shifted. "Here, you want to hold him?"

With trembling hands, Nacho took the bird. He seemed to be holding his breath.

Sarah asked, "You okay?"

A tear dropped onto Nacho's hand. He sniffled.

Marco set a hand on his shoulder. "What's wrong?"

Nacho's brown eyes glittered with tears. "There used to be five billion of these. Did you know that?"

Marco met Sarah's gaze. She swallowed. So many. It seemed impossible that there could be none left.

"Their flocks could be a mile wide and take hours, sometimes days, to fly overhead." Mesmerized, Nacho watched the bird.

Sarah tried to get him off the subject so they could finish what they needed to do. "Leo used the progenitor to make other extinct animals too."

Nacho snapped out of his reverie. "Like what?"

Leo pointed at the ceiling. "Madeira and Xerces butterflies. Tasmanian tigers—"

Nacho shook his head. "This can't be happening."

Sarah smiled. "It is."

Leo said, "Now let's put this bird away and get the butterflies."

Once the butterflies were caught and carefully put away, the only two empty modules left were the ones that had held Nacho and Ahab.

Leo said, "The last two signals will arrive within the hour."

Sarah gulped. "What happens then?"

"Best case, if the modules are all full, my ship will leave automatically."

"And if they aren't?" asked Nacho.

"They will be," said Marco firmly. "I promised they would. But we need to get back to the beach, fast. Come on." He started toward the dark passage.

"Wait," said Leo. "There's a faster way."

Sarah gripped Ahab's collar. They entered the narrow white hallway. Ahab's nails clicked on the shiny, glittery tile. They walked past several doors, and Sarah recognized the one with the machine that made the food. She could almost smell that grilled cheese and wanted so badly to tell Nacho about it. But she knew there wasn't enough time. They went down another pristine white corridor, and Leo opened another set of doors.

Sarah led Ahab through into a clear circular space nearly a quarter mile across. The ceiling gave way to blue sky. "What is this place?"

Leo said, "The center of the volcano."

"Hold on. This volcano is real?" asked Marco.

"Very. It was far smaller when we arrived. But we helped it along, made it the size it is now to cloak our ship. And also stabilized it." He frowned.

"What?" Marco asked.

"Well, once the ship leaves, the volcano may become unstable. And if it does . . . there's no telling when it will erupt."

Nacho asked, "Should we be worried??"

Leo started to say something, but Marco cut him off. "You *grew* a volcano. How is that possible?"

Sarah let out half a laugh. "How is any of this possible?"

"True," muttered Marco. "So how are we getting to the beach?"

Leo pointed behind Sarah.

A sleek oblong silver craft sat in shadow.

Nacho gasped. "Is that a flying saucer?"

"That's our shuttle," said Leo.

"Why didn't you just go back to your ship in that?" asked Marco.

"Can't," said Leo. "Power comes from this annex ship and the shuttle won't operate if it's more than ten thousand miles away. Plus . . ."

"You wanted to finish what your grandfather started," said Sarah.

Tears welled up in Leo's eyes.

She touched his arm. "You're almost done."

With the back of a webbed hand, Leo brushed away the tears. He walked over to the shuttle and touched the side.

The clear top lifted completely, hovering six feet in the air.

"Whoa . . . ," said Nacho.

Leo said, "Plenty of room."

Sarah patted the metal side, which tingled under her fingers. "Come on, boy!" Ahab jumped in and turned to face her, tail wagging. Sarah pulled herself up and hooked a leg over the side.

"You need help?" asked Marco.

"Nope." She rolled over and in, then sat next to the dog on a white seat covered with a slick, silvery fabric.

Nacho followed, after a boost from Marco. He plopped down next to Sarah and Ahab and then smacked his hand on his forehead. "Oh no! I forgot my backpack."

"We don't have time." Marco climbed in and sat down in front. "Sorry."

Nacho sighed. "It's fine."

Finally, Leo climbed in and took the pilot's seat directly facing a console. The top closed down over them.

Sarah started to sweat. She felt like she couldn't breathe. "Are you sure you know how to drive this thing?"

As if to answer, Leo swiped a hand over the panel. The controls lit up, beeping and flashing. He muttered, "We're about to find out."

Fresh, cool air rushed over them. Sarah took a deep breath.

The craft lifted, rocking unsteadily from side to side.

"Whoa!" cried Nacho.

Ahab whined.

Sarah set a trembling hand on his head. "It's okay, boy." At least she hoped it was.

They rose farther in the air.

Sarah peeked out and watched the floor recede. Her heart pounded faster.

Nacho grabbed her free hand and squeezed.

"Are you scared?" she whispered.

"I should be." He grinned. "But this is *way* too cool."

Sarah stared up through the roof.

The blue sky got closer and closer.

At last, Sarah stared out at the craggy lip of the volcano. They paused there, hovering, even with the top.

Marco whistled. "Whoa. Check it out."

Sarah took a deep breath and got up on her knees to look down. She gasped. From their height, everything was visible: the beach, the beautiful lagoon, and the tops of the trees.

"Hold on!" said Leo.

Sarah grabbed Ahab with one hand, the back of Marco's seat with the other.

With a jolt, they sped forward. The green and blue and white of the sand became a blur underneath.

BOOM!

The craft tipped to the right, and Ahab and Nacho both tumbled onto Sarah.

"Ow!" Sarah pushed at them and managed to get them both off her. "What happened?"

They swayed again, the other way, and she fell on Nacho. She sat back up.

"Leo!" Marco pointed straight ahead.

Leo's hands waved across the console, trying to smooth out their ride. "I can't look right now!"

But Sarah could.

Red streaks in the sky swirled together, working quickly as they stitched together a crimson orb.

"Oh no," she whispered.

"It's coming!" yelled Nacho.

The latest red ball hurtled straight toward them.

"Get out of the way!" yelled Marco.

"I'm trying!" Leo pushed a button and twirled a knob.

Marco jabbed to his right. "Go to the side! To the side!"

"I only know how to go forward and up!"

Sarah's stomach did somersaults. The ball came closer and closer, red vapor trailing. "Now would be a good time to figure it out!"

Marco pointed at a red button on the console. "What about that?"

Leo shook his head. "I don't know!"

"I don't care!" Marco pushed it.

Sarah smashed into the seat in front of her.

The craft was at a complete standstill, frozen in the air.

The crimson orb was nearly upon them.

"Go!" cried Marco.

Leo slammed his hand down on a black button.

The top of Sarah's head hit the ceiling as they dropped out of the air. "OW!"

She glanced up.

The red orb flashed past, mere inches above her face. She started to sigh with relief, but her stomach lurched.

"We're dropping!" yelled Nacho.

Leo arrested their fall abruptly, sending Sarah into the ceiling once again. "Come *on*."

They were even with the treetops.

Sarah smacked the window. "Let me out of this stupid thing. I'd rather walk!"

"Sorry." Leo turned around. "Is everyone okay?"

Nacho and Marco both rubbed their heads.

Ahab lay down between Sarah and Nacho, rested

his snout on his paws, and whined. His huge eyes blinked at Sarah.

She leaned down and kissed his head. "Sorry, boy."

Leo said, "I think I've almost got it figured out . . ."

Sarah rolled her eyes and set a hand on her smarting head as well. *"Awesome."*

Leo studied the panel.

"How much time do you have?" asked Marco.

"There's only one ball left. About half an hour in your time."

Sarah frowned. "Then why are we sitting here?"

"I think this is it . . ." Leo touched a button and the ship sped forward.

All the green outside was simply a blur to Sarah. The speed made her queasy. She set a hand on her belly. Do not hurl, do not hurl. But she had to admit that even if she did get sick, the ride was way better than a hot walk and getting chased by freaks of nature.

Within a few moments, Leo slowed. "Tell me where to land."

Sarah's shoulders slumped, and she leaned back with a sigh.

Marco waved his hand. "Here! Our beach is just around the corner." He grasped the tube.

Leo lowered the ship and landed with a jolt on the beach.

Nacho leaned over and whispered to Sarah, "He needs to work on his landings."

Sarah added, "And on his *flying* in general."

The top lifted.

Sarah clambered out. She resisted the overwhelming urge to drop to her knees and kiss the sand.

Ahab needed no coaxing and bounded off, tail wagging.

"Ahab, no no no." Sarah tried to catch him, but he was out of reach. "Marco, help!"

Marco leaped out of the ship and onto the sand. He lunged for the dog, but missed. "He's going toward our camp. We'll catch up to him."

Nacho hopped down beside Sarah, and Leo followed them down the beach after Ahab, who was about a hundred yards ahead.

Then the dog disappeared.

"What if he went to the camp?" asked Sarah.

Marco said, "He'll be fine."

A few minutes later they reached the corner with the embankment that led to their beach.

"Here's the plan." Marco faced them and held up the tube. "I hit Fox's girlfriend with this before she has a chance to pull the gun." He glanced at Leo. "Then we get her and her dog back to your cave. And you are free to leave."

"You make it sound so easy," said Leo.

"A little *too* easy, probably."

Sarah gasped and whirled around.

"Well, look at all you small persons." Miss Blackstone stood there, one hand firmly gripping Ahab's collar, the dog panting next to her. The other hand held the gun, pointed at his head. "Now, if you care at all for this dog, someone better tell me where Laird is. Pronto."

12

Marco's heart sunk. She had them. His plan would never work now.

But then Miss Blackstone's forehead furrowed as she noticed Leo.

Marco took the opportunity to casually sidestep, so that he was halfway hidden by Leo. He tucked his arm with the tube behind his back.

Even if she'd caught sight of the weapon, Miss Blackstone had no way of knowing its function. He snuck a glance out at the sailboat.

He squinted, searching for a sign that John had called for help.

Nothing.

No red.

Had John not been able to call for help? That would be a setback, but they could still get off the island by themselves, especially with Fox out of the picture. Or maybe there simply wasn't anything red available. Or what if John hadn't made it to the boat.

No, that can't be. Marco ignored that one and focused on the first two, much brighter possibilities. He had to have made it. He had to.

Miss Blackstone tightened her hold on Ahab. "Where's Laird? Well? Start talking."

No one said anything.

She rolled her eyes and jerked her head at Leo. "You. Odd-looking child. Where is Fox?"

"He's with his treasure," said Sarah.

Heads swung toward her. Marco bit his lip. Oh, Sarah, be careful. . . .

Sarah set her hands on her hips. "It's too heavy to drag here. He needs you to come to him."

Miss Blackstone's lips pursed. "And just how does he expect me to do *that*?"

Sarah pointed at Sarge's sail. "Sail around to the other end and pick him up."

Marco sucked in a breath. Whether or not Miss

Blackstone bought it, she was considering it, which meant she was definitely distracted. He leaned closer to Leo and nudged him in the back with the tube.

Without turning around, Leo slowly took hold of the weapon.

"Why should I believe you?" Miss Blackstone lifted a foot and sand trickled out of her sandal.

Sarah held her arms out to the sides. "Do you *really* think he would come back without the treasure?"

Miss Blackstone lowered the gun. "Well, I don't *know* what that idiot was thinking."

Leo lifted the tube.

Miss Blackstone whipped the gun up. "Freeze, you little freak."

"She's quicker than she looks," whispered Nacho.

The woman turned to Sarah. "It's time to stop with your little fibs. All of you, get up there. Slowly! And, you, drop that white thing, whatever it is."

Leo bent down and set the tube on the sand.

"Go on!" Miss Blackstone waved the gun. "Single file!"

Leo started to round the corner and shot Marco a worried glance.

Nacho tripped on a piece of driftwood and fell to his knees.

"Oh, come on," huffed Miss Blackstone. "This isn't difficult."

"Leave him alone!" snapped Sarah.

Miss Blackstone grabbed one of Sarah's braids and yanked.

"OW!" Sarah tried to get away, but the woman had too good a grip.

"Get your hands off *her*!"

Yvonna stood on the top of the dune, eyes narrowed, hands on her hips. Her dark hair blew out behind her as the skirt of her pink dress fluttered in the breeze. She took one long step and leaped. She landed right on Miss Blackstone and knocked her to the sand.

They rolled over and then over again.

The gun slipped out of Miss Blackstone's hand and slid down the bank.

Sarah ran over and picked it up.

Marco said, "Careful with—"

Sarah pitched it straight into the ocean and wiped her hands on her shorts. She raised her eyebrows at Marco.

The two women continued to struggle in the sand. Miss Blackstone's sunglasses were askew, and red lipstick had smeared down her left cheek.

Nacho's mouth fell open. "I guess Mom's feeling better."

Leo grabbed the white tube and aimed it at Miss Blackstone. But with the two women grappling, there was no clear shot.

With a grunt, Yvonna pinned Miss Blackstone to the ground. "Don't you *ever* speak to my children like that. In fact, don't even look at them."

Marco and Sarah ran over to help Yvonna hold Miss Blackstone as she struggled. Marco asked Leo, "What was in that medicine anyway?"

Leo shrugged.

Marco said, "We need to let Leo shoot her."

"What?" The women spoke in unison and noticed Leo for the first time. Both stared at him.

Nacho said, "Mom, meet Leo. He's an alien."

Yvonna raised her eyebrows. "I thought I'd dreamed that conversation about the spaceship."

"It was true," said Sarah. "Leo can help. And we can help him."

Marco's mom asked, "What do you want me to do?"

"Let her go on three." Leo aimed the tube.

Sarah stepped away from Miss Blackstone, who cried out, "Wait!"

Leo said, "One. Two. Three!"

Marco and his mom jumped up.

Leo fired.

To her credit, Miss Blackstone struggled longer than Fox had. But she soon succumbed to the net and lay there, a heaving white lump on the sand.

"Good shot," said Yvonna.

Sarah smiled. "She should be happy. It matches her outfit."

"Now, where's her dumb dog?" asked Marco.

"Bentley? He actually bit her and she tied him up." Yvonna's eyes widened. "Oh! Cash and Sarge!"

Nacho said, "I'll get them loose! Come on, Leo." They climbed the bank and disappeared.

Marco hugged his mom. "I'm so glad you're better."

"Me too." She held him for a moment before she spread one arm out to Sarah. "Sweetie?"

With no hesitation, Sarah stepped in and hugged her stepmother's waist. "I was so worried."

"I know. *Now,*" she asked Sarah, "where is your father?"

Sarah shrugged. "Marco saw him last."

Marco's gaze drifted to the sailboat.

"He swam out there?" asked his mom.

"Yeah." He didn't add that the sharkodile was still out there and he hadn't actually seen John make it.

Sarge and Cash jogged down the beach. Nacho and Leo followed, a small white lump tucked under one of Leo's arms.

"Well." Sarge stared down at Miss Blackstone. "She finally stopped talking."

Leo said, "I have to leave."

Sarge kept glancing at Leo's gills. "So everything Cash told me is true?" He set an arm around her shoulders.

Cash nodded. "Here's my proof."

Marco said, "Leo has to get back to his ship." He pointed at Miss Blackstone. "With her and the dog."

"I'll need help," said Leo.

"I'll go," said Marco.

"No way," said his mom. "None of you are leaving my sight again."

Sarge stepped up. "I could go."

Marco shook his head. "I think . . . I think you need to check the boat and make sure it's ready to go." Just in case they needed to make a quick exit. He faced his mom. "You have to let me go help Leo. I promised him."

His mom said, "No."

"I'll go too," said Sarah.

"Oh, come on, you two!" Marco's mom threw up her hands. "*You've* been running around." She gestured at Sarge and Cash. "*They've* been tied up." She flopped a wrist toward the water. "John is who knows where." She shook her head. "We're going to the boat, now, *all of us*. That's final."

Marco held up a hand as she started to protest. "Mom, I made a deal with Leo. I promised to help him get home if he did something for me. And he did."

His mom's gaze drifted to Leo. "What did he do?"

"He gave us medicine," said Sarah.

Marco said, "I gave it to you."

"And you got better," said Cash. "Like, right away."

Marco raised his eyebrows at her. "Really?"

Cash said, "Right after you left. I watched her."

His mom's shoulders slumped. "Seriously?"

"Mom, please? We had a deal. You have to let me help him."

"Fine." She raised her palms. "But you better be back here—"

"We will!" Marco turned to Sarge. "Can you help us get her into the shuttle?"

"The what?" Sarge asked.

Nacho said, "It's a spaceship!"

Cash raised her eyebrows at him.

"We can stand here talking about it," said Marco. "Or we can just show you."

"All right," said Yvonna. "Show us."

13

Sarah watched Sarge and Marco pick up Miss Blackstone. Leo carried the dog, and the rest walked behind
them to the shuttle.

Sarge whistled when he saw it. "This is unbelievable."

He lifted Miss Blackstone inside, then climbed into
the seat behind the console.

"That's my seat," said Leo.

Sarge held up a finger. "Just give a man one minute
here, okay?" He sat there, smiling and shaking his head.
"Unbelievable."

Cash ran a hand along the slick sides. Yvonna joined
her for a moment and then frowned at Marco. "Are you
sure this thing is safe?"

Sarah widened her eyes at Marco.

He ignored her. "Yep. We made it here, didn't we?"

Yvonna slanted her eyes at him, looking a tad skeptical.

"Mom, it's fine. Really."

"We need to go," said Leo.

Sarge sighed, patted the console, and then hopped down to the sand.

Leo took his place.

Then Marco hopped up and Sarah started to follow.

Yvonna said, "Sarah, you should stay here."

"No way." Sarah shook her head. "I'm going to help see this through."

Ahab barked.

Sarah hugged him. "Boy, you have to stay."

Cash walked over and grabbed his collar. "I'll take care of him."

Sarah asked her, "You promise?"

Cash smiled. "Of course."

"Okay. Be back soon." Sarah ran and jumped up, rolling over the side and onto the seat. She found herself face-to-face with the mummy-wrapped Miss Blackstone.

"Yikes." Sarah quickly scooted over to the side.

"Wait for me!" Nacho yelled.

His mom grabbed his arm. "Oh, no way."

"But, Mom!"

"I'm keeping at least one of you close."

The top of the shuttle closed over them, and the craft lifted steadily into the air. Leo circled back toward the cave.

Sarah looked down at the island. Were they almost free of it?

All they had to do was put Miss Blackstone and the dog in the modules and then Leo could leave.

And then so could the rest of them.

Home! Sarah smiled. She'd begun to think they'd never make it back.

The shuttle lurched.

"What's wrong?" asked Marco.

Sarah dropped to her knees and leaned forward between the two front seats. A red light flashed on the console.

Leo set a hand over it, but it didn't stop.

"Is there a problem?" Sarah crossed her fingers and hoped that there wasn't.

"I don't know." Leo swiped his hand over the light again.

The craft began to buck and lost several dozen feet of altitude. "I think that it is low on power."

"But we're so close to your ship," said Marco.

"I know," said Leo. "But it hasn't been used since my grandfather got back from his last trip. I don't think he charged it back up."

"Are you *kidding* me? A *spaceship* that has to be *charged*?" Sarah groaned. "What kind of aliens are you anyway?"

Marco pointed ahead. "We're almost to the volcano."

Leo shook his head. "I don't think I can make it up there. We'll have to land at the cave entrance."

"Where we came in before?" asked Marco.

"No." Leo pointed ahead. "The larger one I led you out of." The shuttle slowed, bucking so much that Sarah had to hold on.

Leo steered the craft to the sand, where they landed with a bump.

Sarah sighed. At least the landing was smoother than the last time. "Are you sure this is where we came out?"

"Yes, it's right there," said Leo.

Sarah still couldn't see the entrance. Obviously Leo kept this one cloaked much better than the other.

Marco glanced at Miss Blackstone and the dog. "We'll have to carry them."

The top of the shuttle slowly rose. "No," said Leo. "Stay here and I'll be right back with the skimmer."

Sarah and Marco exchanged a glance. Skimmer?

The alien boy dropped to the ground and jogged into the cave.

Marco jumped down and Sarah moved to the front. She leaned over. "How are we going to get back?"

Marco tapped the side of the shuttle. "Hopefully he can give this thing enough of a charge to give us a ride."

Sarah studied the western sky. Nothing but blue, no streaks of red in sight.

As if he'd read her mind, Marco said, "We've got plenty of time. Five minutes to get them into the modules, another five to run us back. That puts Leo back here and ready to go with fifteen to spare."

Sarah bit her lip. She hoped it would all be that simple.

"Whoa!" Marco grinned. "Check it out."

Leo sped out of the entrance on a floating silver-slatted platform about the size of a large picnic table. Leo held on to the silver control stick that jutted straight up from the front. The platform lowered until it hovered at Sarah's eye level.

"So that's a skimmer?" asked Marco.

"We use it for hauling things around the annex." Leo pointed. "Let's get them inside."

Marco climbed back into the shuttle, and he and

Sarah dragged Miss Blackstone onto the skimmer. Marco picked up the dog and set him on it too.

"Remember my weapon," said Leo.

Marco tucked the tube under one arm.

Leo hopped into the shuttle and inserted a glowing blue tab into the console. "This will charge it. Let's go." Leo got back on the skimmer and held out a webbed hand. Sarah took it and stepped across the gap of space between the two.

The platform wobbled slightly as she stepped down.

Marco jumped on, and the entire thing tipped.

"Hey!" Sarah held out her hands, feeling like she was surfing.

"Careful," said Leo. "You might want to sit."

Sarah sat down in the middle. She tried not to touch Miss Blackstone and wished there was something to hang on to.

Marco plopped on the edge. His legs dangling as he held the tube. "This is awesome! How fast does it go?"

Leo didn't answer. He pushed forward on the stick and they entered the passageway with the stone floors, lit by torches on the walls. The temperature dropped several degrees.

The corridor was wide enough to accommodate them at first, then grew smaller.

Leo nearly scraped one side. Marco yanked his legs up just in time.

In a few moments, they reached the cavern.

Leo lowered the skimmer to the floor right in front of the two empty modules. He carried Bentley to one and set him inside. "Marco, can you free him?"

Marco twisted the tube and freed Bentley, who began to yap.

Leo quickly locked the module. Mist filled the space.

All three of them carried Miss Blackstone to the one remaining module and dragged her inside.

Sarah took a moment to catch her breath. "What will happen to her? And Fox?"

Leo said, "Well, they'll stay in here for now. Like all the animals."

"But when you reach your planet?" Sarah didn't want to see Fox or Miss Blackstone ever again. But she needed to know. "What will you do with them?"

Leo said, "They will be allowed to stay on my planet, of course. We'll take care of them."

"Really?" asked Marco. "Even though Fox stole your progenitor?"

Leo frowned. "Or maybe we'll keep them frozen for a while."

"Will that hurt them?" asked Sarah.

"No, it's like they're sleeping. Besides, it won't be up to me. It'll be up to the elders."

"I don't want anything bad to happen to them." Sarah sighed. "But I think our planet will be better off without them."

Leo asked Marco, "Ready?"

"Yeah." Marco twisted the tube. The white net dissipated.

Miss Blackstone raised a red talon at them. "You little miscreants better get me out of here, *now*!" She gave them one last, cruel look before she froze.

Sarah watched the mist rise up around her, frost appearing on the glass door.

"Wow," said Marco. "Is it really done?"

Leo glanced at the lights on the bottom of the modules, now an unblinking green. He grinned. "We did it!"

The three stood there in a circle.

Sarah realized this was the last time they'd be together. Leo had to go back to his ship and his family.

And she and Marco had to go back to theirs.

But it wasn't easy to say good-bye to the alien boy.

Sarah looked away, but her gaze went straight to Nacho's backpack. "Hey!"

Leo picked it up. "He'll want this back, I think."

Marco noticed the trunk, which was still where

Sarah and Leo had dropped it. "What are you going to do with that?"

Leo frowned. "Wait here a moment." He went around the divider.

Marco ran his fingers over the carvings on the trunk. "It would have been cool to have."

"What if you hadn't pulled it off the *Moonflight*?" asked Sarah.

Marco shrugged. "We'd be gaining an alien step-brother about now, I guess."

Sarah laughed.

Marco grinned.

Leo came back with the backpack. "I'll trade you."

Marco gave him the white tube and took the backpack. "Whoa!" He nearly dropped it. "It's so heavy."

Leo's gaze drifted from Marco to Sarah. "I can't take both parts of the progenitor with me."

Sarah glanced at the trunk. "Weren't they both in there?"

Leo shook his head. "I slipped half out while Fox wasn't looking."

"Wait." Marco frowned. "Why do you want to leave it with *us*?"

"I trust you," said Leo. "And we don't need it anymore."

Sarah took in the sweep of modules. "But what if you need to make something else?"

Leo sighed and looked around the cavern. "If we can't rebuild our world with all of this, then we don't deserve it. Plus, it's too much of a risk to have both parts. The same thing that destroyed our world the first time . . ." He trailed off. "Better to remove that possibility."

Sarah said, "You can always come back, you know. If you want to visit."

"I'll keep that in mind." Leo smiled. "Now let me take you back. I have just enough time." He tucked the tube under his arm.

Sarah took a last look around the cavern, knowing she would never see it again. Knowing that no one on the planet would ever see it again. All these modules, all these animals; she truly hoped that Leo and his people made it back to their planet to start again.

She had to smile.

They had done it.

They had survived; they'd helped Leo go home.

And now they had to go home.

"Oh no," whispered Marco.

Sarah turned.

Mere steps in front of her, halfway to the entrance of the corridor, Leo and Marco stood motionless.

Blocking their way was the black panther with the red beard.

Sarah slapped a hand over her mouth.

The feline's red tail swished slowly from side to side as it growled low in its throat and bared sharp white teeth. The animal crouched, like it was preparing to pounce.

14

Marco's heartbeat raced. He glanced around, hoping for some brilliant escape plan. But modules lay behind them, the cavern walls were all around them, and the nearest escape was blocked by the panther.

The other passageway was too far; they'd never make it before the cat would be on them. Well, one of them—the others might make it.

But Marco wasn't willing to risk either Leo or Sarah.

So he stood his ground. He'd have to come up with something else.

The panther growled louder.

"It's going to attack," whispered Sarah.

"Shoot it, Leo!" said Marco.

Leo stood there, eyes wide, mouth open.

Marco whispered as loudly as he could. "Leo! Shoot it."

But Leo was still paralyzed.

"Marco," whispered Sarah. "There's an empty module back here."

Marco slowly turned his head. The module was about five yards from Sarah, fifteen yards from him and Leo, about the same distance they were from the cat. Could they make it?

Marco swallowed. They had to try. "Leo, we're going to start backing up."

Finally Leo blinked and met Marco's gaze. The boy's eyes were full of tears.

Marco realized that he must be thinking about how his grandfather had died. Maybe he was reliving that horrible moment, the last time that he had come face-to-face with the cat. And the time before that, when he had tried to shoot the panther with the tube and failed.

"This time will be different, Leo," he said. "We'll get out of this."

Leo blinked and went back to staring at the panther, which hadn't come any closer.

"Sarah," whispered Marco. "Back toward the module—"

"No," said Leo at full volume.

The panther's ears twitched.

"Don't make it mad," whispered Marco. "Let's just back up and go in the module and—"

"And what?" Leo's eyes locked on the panther as he spoke to Marco. "Hide in there until time has run out?"

"You're running out of time. The modules are full, and your ship is going to leave. . . ." Marco's words trailed off as he realized what he was saying. Yes, the ship would take off.

But he and Sarah would still be on it.

"*You* are the ones running out of time, Marco." Leo tightened his grip on the tube and aimed at the panther.

The panther snarled and twitched its scarlet tail.

"Marco!" whispered Sarah. "Come on."

"It's going to attack," said Marco.

Leo fired.

Nothing happened.

Marco's stomach clenched.

Crouching, the panther screamed and leaped off its hind legs.

"Leo!" yelled Marco.

Suddenly the skimmer flew over Marco's head with Sarah holding the control stick. She caught the midsection of the panther with the edge of the platform a second before it reached Leo.

The panther dug into the slats with long front claws, its back half hanging off as Sarah careened around the cavern. "What do I do?" she yelled. "Get that thing off!"

Leo shifted his aim.

"More to the left," said Marco.

"Got it," said Leo. The net blasted out toward the cat.

"Direct hit!" yelled Marco.

The cat slipped from the skimmer, landed and rolled, then came to stop, a crumpled white heap.

Sarah still circled in the skimmer, her eyes huge. "How do I land this thing?"

"Back and down to the left!" called Leo.

Finally, the skimmer scraped the floor of the cavern, jolting to a stop. Sarah asked, "Is the cat hurt?"

Marco nudged it gently with his toe. "No, he's just immobilized."

Leo dropped the tube and leaned over, webbed hands on his knees, breathing hard.

Marco set a hand on his back. "You did it!"

"What will you do with it?" asked Sarah.

Leo shrugged. "I'll figure that out later."

Marco and Sarah exchanged a glance. He put both straps of the backpack over his shoulders. "We've gotta go."

Leo stepped onto the skimmer. "Move aside."

With no argument, Sarah plopped down in the middle and Marco jumped aboard. He knelt at the same time that Leo jammed the control stick forward. They sped through the corridor, no one saying a word.

The fires in the torches flickered as they flew by.

By Marco's calculations, there was still plenty of time. Hopefully the shuttle was charged enough so that Leo could zip them all the way to the *Moonflight* and make it back himself.

Sarah hugged her knees to her chest and stared straight ahead.

Finally, they reached the entrance and Leo brought the craft to a halt on the ground just outside. Sarah jumped off and Marco followed.

The ground shook under their feet.

"Marco!" Sarah pointed to the western sky, streaks of red swirling.

"The last one," said Leo.

Marco whirled to face him. "You can take us back, right? There's still time!"

Leo's mouth dropped open.

"Maybe not," said Sarah.

Marco slowly turned back.

The crimson swirls in the sky had turned into not one, not two, but three orbs. All twirled for a moment, as if steeling themselves.

"Why are there three?" asked Sarah.

The red balls shot forward as if launched from a cannon, heading right for them.

"Look out!" Marco grabbed Sarah's arm and dragged her back toward the cave. They ran inside with Leo beside them and sprinted about thirty yards down the passage.

BOOM!

The explosion knocked them forward.

Marco landed, skidding forward on his chest. He quickly rolled over, wincing at his skinned knees and arms.

Leo and Sarah lay on the ground beside him.

Marco asked, "You guys okay?"

Leo got up and brushed himself off. "Yes."

Sarah sat up. She pushed stray hairs out of her face and frowned at her skinned hands. "Close enough."

A beeping started up, so loud that Sarah covered her ears and Marco had to yell to be heard. "What is that?"

Leo's eyes grew big. He grabbed Marco and Sarah

and tried to pull them up. "Come on! You have to get out!"

"Why?!" Sarah got to her feet beside Marco.

Leo yelled something, but Marco couldn't hear him. Then the alien pointed.

The top of the exit seemed to be shrinking. What had been an eight-foot-tall hole was now seven.

Marco blinked. Was he seeing things?

The space narrowed more.

Their exit, now at only a clearance of six feet, was slowly disappearing.

"Run!" Marco grabbed Sarah's hand.

Five feet.

"We're not gonna make it!" Sarah let go of Marco's hand and they both pumped their arms and raced.

Four feet and closing.

Marco's heart pounded.

They were only five yards away. "Almost there!" The backpack slipped off one of Marco's shoulders. He reached out to catch it and stumbled.

He hit the ground on one knee just as Sarah bent nearly double and scooted through the opening.

Three feet.

"Marco!" Sarah's eyes were huge circles. She fell to her knees and slapped the ground. "Hurry!"

Two feet.

"Come on!"

Marco took a deep breath, pushed off his one leg, and dove forward. He hit the ground.

A sharp jolt of pain shot through his lower arm. He groaned and rolled over. His lower half was still inside the cave.

"I've got you!" Sarah grabbed him by the backpack and dragged him until they were clear of the descending rock.

"Leo!" cried Sarah.

Leo was inside. He dropped to his knees as the opening closed to one foot.

"Get out!" yelled Sarah.

"He can't." Marco reached up and set a hand on her arm. "That's his ride."

Leo lay down, his head on the ground. One webbed hand raised in a wave. His lizard eyes blinked and glittered.

Marco lifted his hand in return.

"Bye, Leo," Sarah said.

The rock dropped all the way with a thud that reverberated under them.

Leo was gone.

The beeping hushed.

"That's it?" Sarah's eyes were full of tears.

Marco felt a lump in his throat. "We knew this would happen. This is what we *wanted* to happen." He sat up with a groan, cradling his arm.

"Are you okay?" asked Sarah.

"Just landed on it hard. I'm fine." But his arm hurt.

With no warning, Sarah flung her arms around Marco. "I thought you weren't going to make it."

Marco hugged her back with his good arm for a moment, then leaned away and cleared his throat. "You could have just left me, you know."

"Thought about it." A corner of her mouth turned up. "But I didn't feel like getting grounded for life."

The ground trembled under him.

On instinct, Marco's gaze shot to the west.

The sky was blue, free of any red swirls.

"What's happening?" asked Sarah.

Marco started to get to his feet. But the ground shook so much that Marco nearly lost his balance.

Sarah helped pull him to standing.

He glanced up. "Look!"

A massive white spaceship, the size of a football stadium and shaped like a sphere, rose up above the top of the volcano.

Marco stared. No words came.

Sarah dug her fingers into his arm.

The ship hovered at the top of the volcano for a moment, so long a moment that Marco began to wonder if something was wrong. But then it lifted, rising so fast that it suddenly disappeared.

All was still, save for their ragged breathing from the rapid escape.

Marco turned to Sarah. "It's over."

"Then why do I still feel sad?"

"Because it's always hard to say good-bye." Marco glanced up at the sky again. He didn't know what he was expecting to see, but there was nothing other than the blue sky. A wisp of a cloud appeared, spiraling up. "That's a weird . . ."

"What?"

"I was just going to say that's a weird cloud, but—" The spiral of white grew thicker and grayer. Marco's gaze drifted along to the bottom, which seemed to precisely adjoin the top of the volcano.

Sarah said, "Are we *sure* that's a cloud?"

The ground rumbled. Different from what was caused by the orbs or Leo's ship. This disturbance came from *far* beneath them.

"That volcano is gonna blow. It's time to go," Marco said. He glanced once more at the top of the volcano, where the wispy spiral had become downright thick and gray and sinister. "We need to get back, like, now."

"We have a little problem," Sarah said.

Marco turned around.

The shuttle was a charred, blackened heap, the smoking remains of one of the red orbs directly on top of it.

They had just lost their ride back.

15

"Oh no." Sarah's hopes evaporated as she took in the wrecked shuttle. On foot, they would never make it back in time. This couldn't be how it ended, could it?

Then her gaze went to the skimmer. "There! Come on!"

Marco moved a bit slowly with his bad arm, but clambered aboard.

Sarah positioned herself in front of the silver stick.

"Don't you think I should drive?" asked Marco.

Sarah scowled at him. "You're hurt. I can do it."

Marco raised his eyebrows. "You didn't do that great the first time."

"Well, there's a learning curve, obviously." She grabbed the stick and pulled back. They shot straight up about six feet. She shrieked and pushed the stick away from her. Immediately they zoomed forward and headed straight for a thick palm tree.

"Sarah! Look out!"

Sarah leaned to the left, drawing the stick along with her. The skimmer swerved and circled back.

Marco said, "Just stop! Can you stop?"

"I'm trying!" Sarah pulled the stick slowly back to center and the craft hovered. She took a deep breath. "I think I've got it now."

"Maybe we should just walk," said Marco.

He was right. She had hoped the second time around would make the skimmer easier to fly, but she wasn't any better. And the time they would save wasn't worth crashing. "Let me set this down." She started to lower the skimmer.

BOOM!

Sarah froze.

Overhead, dark smoke poured from the top of the volcano. Bright orange bits shot into the air as a thick stream of glowing lava flowed over the edges.

Sarah clamped her hands down on the stick and steered the craft around to face their camp. "Hold on!" She nudged the controller forward.

The skimmer surged.

They buzzed smoothly along the beach, halfway between the tree line and the water. Sarah relaxed a little as the wind blew her braids back. She couldn't help but smile. "It's like a flying carpet!"

"It's not so bad." Marco grinned. "Just don't go any faster."

"I got this," said Sarah.

A faint *meow* came from the trees.

"Do you hear that?" called Marco.

"Is that the kitten Cash heard?" asked Sarah.

"I don't think so. Look!"

A brown monkey swung from the branches, first reaching out with a long tail, then spindly arms, keeping perfect pace with the skimmer. The creature turned its head toward them, revealing the face of a massive orange tabby cat with blinking green eyes, pink nose, and long white whiskers.

Sarah stared.

"Watch out!" yelled Marco.

Mere inches below them, the rhinocorn bolted out of the trees, followed by the kangaroo with lion's paws and over a dozen other animals of various colors and sizes right behind it.

"Go up!"

Sarah yanked back on the controller and clung to it

with both hands. They shot up about ten feet. She scrunched her eyes shut and pushed forward slightly.

She opened her eyes.

The skimmer had leveled off. She relaxed and observed the exodus from the trees, an entire herd of freakish creatures. "Where are they going?"

Her stepbrother didn't answer.

She glanced back over her shoulder.

He wasn't there.

"Marco!" she screamed.

At the very end of the platform, fingers gripped a slat. "Hang on!" She managed to bring the craft to a stop in midair and ran to the back.

Marco hung off the skimmer, clinging with only one hand as the other clutched the backpack.

Sarah gasped. "Don't let go!"

The herd of animals galloped and ran and hopped and buzzed right under them, panting and snorting, sand flying up in their wake.

"And don't look down!"

Marco looked down. His legs flailed. "Get me up! Get me up!"

Sarah dropped to her knees and grabbed his wrist.

Marco grunted and thrust the backpack up on the skimmer. He grabbed the platform with that hand.

Sarah leaned back, straining to pull him up. Together they got him onto the skimmer. Marco rolled onto his back, panting and clutching his arm.

"You okay?" asked Sarah.

He took a couple of deep breaths. "I am never riding with you again." But then he grinned at Sarah.

She laughed. "Sorry." She jumped back up and took hold of the controller.

Marco knelt down beside her.

Once again, they were cruising along the sand. They soon caught up to the stampeding animals.

As if to answer her earlier question, Marco said, "They're trying to get as far away from the volcano as possible."

Sarah glanced back. No longer green, the top of the volcano glowed orange. Trees began to topple like dominos, destruction heading toward them.

Trees at their side began to shake, so fast they became green blurs.

Marco said, "I think the whole island is going to collapse."

"Hold on!" Sarah pushed the stick farther forward and they sped up.

Marco pointed. "Our beach is up ahead!"

Sarah said, "Do you think they all got off it?"

"We're about to find out."

Sarge's sailboat came into view, still too far out to see who was on it. Sarah steered toward their beach.

Yvonna stood near the water's edge. She jumped up and down and waved both arms.

"Mom!" Marco yelled. "Go just low enough for her to get on."

Sarah cut a lower path in the air and steered toward her stepmother. Gently, she halted right in front of her, the skimmer hovering a few inches off the sand.

Yvonna said, "I wasn't leaving without you!"

Sarah said, "Get on."

Her stepmother frowned. "Is it safe?"

Marco glanced at Sarah. "Totally," he said.

Yvonna climbed aboard.

"Is everyone else on the boat?" asked Marco.

His mom knelt beside him. "Nacho went with Cash and Sarge."

"My dad?" asked Sarah.

"I sure hope so," said Yvonna.

BOOM!

A fresh bout of lava flew straight into the air.

"Hang on," said Sarah.

"Do you know how to drive this?" asked Yvonna.

"Hold on!" said Marco.

Yvonna grabbed hold of the slats beside her knees.

Sarah pulled the stick back gently and they rose in the air about four feet. She swung them around and pushed the controller forward. The sand receded under them, and then they were over nothing but water.

Ocean spray spit at Sarah's face, cooling her.

Marco called out, "Maybe you should go a little higher."

Sarah glanced at the waves, expecting to see a fin.

Nothing.

Still, she had to force herself to be gentle and not yank as she pulled back on the stick.

They rose another five feet and drew close enough to the sailboat to see Cash and Nacho at the bow, waving.

Sarge was farther back at the wheel.

"I don't see my dad," said Sarah.

The skimmer lurched.

Yvonna shrieked.

"I got it." Sarah pushed the stick forward.

But the skimmer slowed and began to descend. Sarah smacked the controller with an open hand. "Come *on*."

Marco said, "I think this thing is dying."

Sarah glared at him. "Happen to have a charger?"

Marco scowled.

Their descent continued. Sarah pushed the stick as

far forward as it would go. The skimmer limped closer, bit by bit, until it lay only about three feet off the bow of the sailboat, steady in the air but slowly sinking.

Cash and Nacho stood at the rail. He called out, "Jump!"

Marco and Yvonna stood up.

Sarah let go of the stick.

The skimmer immediately began to tilt.

She grabbed it again. "You guys jump. I'll hold it steady."

Marco shook his head. "No, you go. I'll hold it."

"You can't with your arm," said Sarah.

"You're hurt?" asked Yvonna.

"Just get on the boat." Sarah gripped the stick. "This thing is going down."

Marco firmed up the backpack's strap on one shoulder and leaped across the gap. He made it, then turned back to face the skimmer, which sunk slowly toward the water. "Mom, come on!"

Yvonna met Sarah's gaze. "You promise. You'll come right after me."

"Cross my heart," said Sarah. "I'm off this thing as soon as possible."

Yvonna hitched up her pink dress above her knees and leaped across the gap. She landed on the rail and

Marco grabbed her arm. She jumped down to the deck and turned back. "Your turn!"

Suddenly the skimmer listed to one side. Sarah slipped and fell, grabbing on to the stick before she slid all the way off.

"Sarah!" yelled Yvonna.

Breathless, heart pounding, Sarah stuck her feet in slat after slat, scrambling her way up the skimmer until she was high enough to see over the top. About five feet of air lay between her and Yvonna's stricken face.

Sarah hooked one leg over and managed to get up on her knees. Gingerly, she got to her feet, her arms straight out to steady her on the narrow balance-beam edge.

Yvonna leaned over the rail. Sarah held her breath and reached for Yvonna.

"You can do this!" Yvonna leaned out farther.

Sarah pushed off with both her legs, but the skimmer gave slightly, cutting her momentum. But she was already airborne, straining to reach out for Yvonna—

Sarah's fingers brushed the slippery side of the sailboat as she fell.

"Sarah!" yelled Yvonna.

A rope hung down the side of the boat and Sarah managed to snatch it with her right hand. But she slid all the way down, her hand burning. The rest of her body banged into the side of the sailboat. She reached up and held the rope with her other hand.

She clung there, her shoes about a foot above the waves, and stared up.

Yvonna was above, dark hair hanging down as she called to Sarah, "Hold on, sweetie!"

Sarah could do nothing but nod as she hung there, her hands and arms and shoulders screaming from the effort.

Tears leaked out. Where was her dad? Why wasn't he there to save her?

"What is that?" yelled Cash.

A fin was thirty yards away and closing in.

Sarah screamed.

The rope began to slowly raise her.

Not fast enough.

Sarah's burning hands trembled so much she nearly let go of the rope.

Twenty yards.

Sarah dangled there, bumping against the side, going upward inches at a time.

Too slow.

Ten yards.

She was halfway up the side. Still far too close to the water.

Marco yelled, "It's coming!"

The fin neared.

Sarah put one stinging hand above the other and tried to climb.

Nine yards.

Sarah moved her other hand up, barely above the other. Her arms were so tired from hanging on.

Eight yards—

A short distance behind the fin, the water surged and rose up ten feet into the air. A massive red maw of a mouth opened, revealing sharp white teeth at least a foot long.

Sarah screamed.

The mouth clamped down, devoured the shark-odile in one bite, and then disappeared beneath the water.

The resulting wave swamped Sarah and sent her spinning like a top at the end of the rope.

She gasped for breath. Her hands slipped on the drenched rope, and she started to slide.

She was going to fall into the water where that thing would—

Someone grabbed Sarah by her wrist.

She blinked water out of her eyes.

Yvonna hung halfway over the railing. "I've got you." Her eyes fixed on Sarah's. "Focus on me."

Sarah nodded.

Yvonna tightened her grip.

Sarah winced. "Just don't let go."

"I won't." Yvonna yelled, "Pull us up!"

Slowly, slowly, Sarah inched upward, her wrist killing her where her stepmother grasped it. Yvonna disappeared over the top, only her arms still visible at the edge.

Sarah's wrist reached the railing. She lifted her other hand and grabbed on.

Yvonna let go.

Sarah was pulled into a hot, sweaty embrace, encircled by familiar arms.

"Dad." Sarah wrapped her arms around him and buried her face into his damp, dirty shirt. *He* had been the one holding Yvonna. So he *had* been there to help save her, after all. "I'm so glad to see you."

"Same here, kiddo." He pulled back and kissed her forehead. "Are you okay?"

Sarah smiled. "I am now."

"What was that thing?" asked Cash.

Sarah exchanged a glance with Marco. Apparently the sharkodile wasn't the only water mutant Leo and his grandfather had created.

Sarge said, "I'm not sticking around to find out. Everyone on board? Because that, my friends, was our cue to leave."

Sarah's dad set her down on the deck and wrapped a towel around her.

Yvonna hugged Marco. "Where are you hurt?"

Marco held up his arm. "I think I sprained it or something."

"We've got a first-aid kit with some wraps," said Cash. "I'll show you."

She disappeared down into the hold with Marco and Yvonna.

Sarge started the engine and the boat headed out of the lagoon.

Sarah turned toward Shipwreck Island.

The volcano was a black cloud, with momentary glimpses of glowing orange. Half the island was on fire. Sarah could make out the animals at the water's edge. "What's going to happen to them?"

"Look!" said Nacho.

To the west, dark storm clouds had begun to build.

"Maybe it'll rain enough to put out the fire," said Sarah.

Nacho asked, "So Leo left?"

"He did." Sarah noticed the backpack. "Hey, we brought that back."

Nacho took it in both arms and nearly collapsed. "What's in it?"

"Leo left us in charge of half his progenitor."

Nacho set the backpack on the deck and unzipped it. He carefully pulled back the sides, revealing an object wrapped in the white netting. "Should we open it?"

Sarah shook her head. "It's better that we leave it as it is."

Nacho looked disappointed. Then his eyes widened. "What's this?" He pulled out a small parcel wrapped in cloth the color of Leo's jumpsuit. Nacho knelt down and set the cloth on his knees. Slowly he set one corner aside, then another. He gasped.

Two small white eggs lay there.

"What are they?" asked Sarah.

"I think . . ." Nacho trailed off. "But it's not possible."

"What?"

Nacho smiled. "Well, I think, even though it couldn't be . . . I think they're passenger pigeon eggs."

Sarah said, "With Leo? Anything is possible."

Nacho wrapped the eggs back up and carefully tucked them under his shirt, cradling the bulge gently.

Marco came up a moment later, his wrist wrapped in a white bandage.

Yvonna followed behind him and held up a small white tube of cream. "Now for you."

"What's that?" Sarah asked.

"Your hands look like they hurt."

"A little." Sarah held out her rope-burned palms.

Yvonna squeezed out some clear, pungent-smelling ointment and gently rubbed it in. She blew on Sarah's hands and asked, "Better?"

Sarah nodded.

Yvonna winked. "Good." She leaned forward and kissed Sarah's forehead, then went over to Sarah's dad by the railing. They hugged and then he set his hand on her belly.

"And so it starts," said Sarah.

Marco turned away and faced the island with Sarah. "I suppose we should get used to it."

Sarah smiled. "You first."

Marco laughed.

Sarah watched Shipwreck Island grow smaller and smaller. The sun reflected brightly off the water and Sarah squinted. "No one would believe any of this."

"It doesn't matter."

Sarah glanced up at him. "Why do you say that?"

"Well, *we* know it happened. *We* know it's real." He shrugged. "Does it really matter what anyone else thinks?"

"I guess not."

"What's that?" Marco pointed up.

A bird followed them, winging its way closer. Sarah shaded her eyes with a hand. The sun was too bright for her to see the color of the bird, but the outline was impossible to miss. "Are those . . ."

"Four wings? Yeah," Marco said. "Maybe we should keep this between us."

"Definitely," agreed Sarah.

Marco glanced down at his wrist and her hands. "We could shake on it, but . . ."

Sarah grinned.

Sarge called out, "I set a course. Should be to port before dawn."

"This isn't so bad," said Marco.

"The sailboat?" asked Sarah.

Marco shook his head and watched their parents. "Them. Us. This family thing." Before Sarah could say anything, he quickly added, "I'm still *never* riding with you again."

Marco headed toward the hold.

Sarah turned back for one last look at Shipwreck Island.

"Everything okay?" Yvonna stood with her arms around Sarah's dad, both of them smiling, looking like two people who were, no question, absolutely in love.

"Yeah. Everything is just fine." Sarah stepped to the railing and stared up at the sky. More dark clouds headed toward the island. Chances were the fires would be out by dark.

Shipwreck Island became a speck in the distance. Sarah would never forget it, that was for sure. None of them ever would, even once they got back home.

Home.

She watched her dad and Yvonna for a moment as they held each other. Their house would be that now, a home. With all of them. And the new baby.

Sarah smiled. The thought actually didn't seem that bad.

Shouts erupted from below.

Yvonna groaned. "Those boys. I better go see what the problem is."

"No," said Sarah. "I got it." She took one last look at the island where they became a family and went to straighten out her brothers.

THE SHIPWRECK ISLAND SERIES

AN ISLAND OF MYSTERY, STRANGE ANIMALS, TIME TRAVEL, AND TREASURE HAS PLENTY IN STORE FOR THE ROBINSON FAMILY. . . .